The Thing at the Window

On the windowsill, in front of the curtains, a Thing was sitting watching him. Tony thought he would faint with horror. Two small, bloodshot eyes gleamed at him from a deathly pale face framed by tangled hair, which straggled down to a grubby black cape. The figure opened and closed its gaping mouth, grinding its teeth in a totally frightening way, and Tony noticed that these teeth were extremely white and pointed like daggers. Tony's hair stood on end, and his heart practically stopped beating! The Thing at the window was worse than King Kong, worse than Frankenstein, even worse than Dracula. It was the most horrifying apparition Tony had ever seen.

Books by Angela Sommer-Bodenburg

My Friend the Vampire
The Vampire Moves In

Available from MINSTREL BOOKS

MY FRIEND THE VAMPIRE

Angela Sommer-Bodenburg
pictures by Amelie Glienke

A MINSTREL™ BOOK

PUBLISHED BY
SIMON & SCHUSTER, INC.

This book is for Burghardt Bodenburg, whose teeth are so brittle he could never turn into a vampire, and for Ada-Verena Gass, who can make a truly magnificent vampire face, as well as for Katja, who can shout: "Eeek! a vampire!" so beautifully—and for everyone who likes stories about vampires as much as I do.

Angela Sommer-Bodenburg

A MINSTREL BOOK, published by
Simon & Schuster, Inc., 1230 Avenue
of the Americas, New York, New York 10020

This translation copyright © 1982 by Andersen Press Ltd.
First published in German as *Der Kleine Vampir* by Rowohlt
Taschenbuch Verlag, Reinbek bei Hamburg, West Germany
Translated by Sarah Gibson
Cover artwork copyright © 1986 by Amelie Glienke

Published by arrangement with Dial Books for Young Readers,
a Division of E. P. Dutton, Inc.
Library of Congress Catalog Card Number: 83-23930

ISBN: 0-671-55421-2

First Minstrel Books printing July, 1986

10 9 8 7 6 5 4 3 2

A MINSTREL BOOK and colophon are trademarks
of Simon & Schuster, Inc.

Printed in the U.S.A.

1 / The Thing at the Window

It was a Saturday evening, the night when Tony's parents always went out.

"So where are you going tonight?" Tony wanted to know that afternoon. His mother was in the bathroom, busy with her hair curlers.

"Oh," she said, "we'll probably have something to eat, and then we might go dancing."

"What do you mean, *might*?" asked Tony.

"Well, we haven't decided yet," explained his mother. "Is there any reason why it's so important for you to know?"

"No-o," mumbled Tony. He thought it was better not to tell her that he wanted to watch the horror movie on television, which started at eleven o'clock. But it was too late: her suspicions were already aroused.

"Tony," she scolded, turning around so she could look him straight in the eye. "I hope you're not planning to watch something on television."

"Oh, Mom," argued Tony, "what in the world gives you that idea?" Luckily, his mother had turned back to her curlers, and so she did not see how red his face had turned.

"We might even go to the movies," was all she said. "In any case, we probably won't be home before midnight."

Now it was evening, and Tony was alone in the apartment. He lay in bed in his pajamas, with the sheet pulled up to his chin, reading *The Truth About Frankenstein*. The story was about a traveling show. A man in a flowing black cape had just come on the stage to announce the appearance of the monster. Suddenly the alarm clock went off. Tony looked up from his book, frowning at the interruption. Wow, eleven o'clock already! He just had time to turn on the television.

Tony jumped out of bed and pressed the switch. Then he snuggled back beneath the covers and watched as the picture slowly took form on the screen. It was still only a sports show. His room was shadowy and dim; King Kong glowered down from the poster on the wall, his sneer exactly right for Tony's mood. He felt wild and adventurous, as though he were the only survivor of a shipwreck, stranded on a South Sea island inhabited by cannibals. His bed was his hideout, soft and warm, and whenever he wanted to, he could creep in there and be hidden from sight. A heap of provisions lay at the entrance of this den; in fact, the only thing missing was a keg of rum. Tony thought longingly of the bottle of apple juice in the refrigerator; the trouble was, in order to get it, he would have to cross the darkened hallway. Should he swim back to the ship, braving the blood-hungry sharks that were lying in wait for their prey? Tony shivered. But the fact remained that castaways died of thirst much more often than anything else!

So, bravely, he set off. He hated the hallway; the light was permanently broken, and no one bothered to fix it. He hated the coats dangling in the closet, looking like corpses. And then there was the rabbit! He thought with horror of the stuffed animal in his mother's workroom, even though he had enjoyed scaring his friends with it when they came to visit. At last he made it to the kitchen. He took the bottle of apple juice out of the refrigerator and sliced off a large chunk of cheese while he was there. All the time he had half an ear cocked to the other room to make sure the horror movie hadn't started yet. He heard a woman's voice announcing the movie. Tony tucked the bottle under his right arm and hurried back.

However, he had not gone far, just into the hallway, when he noticed that something was not quite right. He stood still and listened . . . and suddenly it dawned on him what was wrong: there wasn't any sound coming from the television! That could mean only one thing: Someone must have sneaked into his room and turned it off! Tony could feel his heart miss a beat and then thud as if it had gone crazy, and a strange lump seemed to move from his tummy to his throat and stick there. Terrible pictures appeared before his eyes, pictures of men with stocking masks, knives, and guns who broke into empty apartments at night to steal, and who would let no one stand in their way. Tony remembered that the window had been left open, and a robber could easily have climbed in over the next-door balcony. All of a sudden there was a crash! The apple juice bottle had slipped from under Tony's arm and had rolled across the hallway, coming to rest by the bedroom door. Tony held his breath and waited . . . but nothing happened. Maybe he was just imagining all this nonsense about robbers. But if that were the case, why had the television stopped?

He picked up the bottle and inched open his bedroom door. The first thing he noticed was a very odd smell, musty and moldering like something in the cellar, but like burning too. Was it coming from the television set? Tony quickly pulled the plug out from the wall and looked to see if the cord was smoldering.

Then Tony heard a strange rattling, which seemed to come from the window. He thought he could make out a shadow behind the curtain, outlined against the bright moonlight. Very slowly, with knees knocking, he forced himself nearer. The strange smell grew stronger, as if someone had been burning a whole box of matches. The rattling was getting louder too. Suddenly Tony froze. On the windowsill, in front of the curtains, which were moving gently in the night breeze, a Thing was sitting watching him. Tony thought he would faint with horror. Two small, bloodshot eyes gleamed at him from a deathly pale face framed by tangled hair, which straggled down to a grubby black cape. The figure opened and closed its gaping mouth, grinding its teeth in a totally frightening way, and Tony noticed that these teeth were extremely white and pointed like daggers. Tony's hair stood on end, and his heart practically stopped beating! The Thing at the window was worse than King Kong, worse than Frankenstein, worse than Dracula even. It was the most horrifying apparition Tony had ever seen.

The Thing seemed to enjoy seeing Tony frightened out of his wits, because it drew its enormous mouth back into a dreadful grin to reveal its needle-sharp, widely spaced teeth more clearly. "A vampire!" gulped Tony.

And the Thing answered in a voice that seemed to come from the bowels of the earth: "But of course I'm a vampire!" It sprang into the room and stood firmly in front of the door. "Are you afraid?" it asked.

Tony could not make a sound.

"You're sort of skinny—not much flesh on you, I'll bet." The vampire looked him up and down. "Where are your parents?"

"At the movies," stammered Tony.

"Aha. Now, let's see. Is your father a healthy type? Would his blood be . . . er, tasty?" The vampire giggled, and its teeth glistened in the moonlight. "As I'm sure you are aware, we vampires live on blood."

"I-I have very b-bad blood," stuttered Tony nervously. "I-I have to t-take pills for it."

"Poor you," growled the vampire, taking a step nearer.

"Don't touch me!" shrieked Tony, attempting to duck. All he managed to do was to knock the end of his bed, and a bag of jelly beans tumbled off onto the floor, the contents spilling out onto the carpet.

The vampire laughed with a rumble that sounded like a peal of thunder. "Well, well! Jelly beans." It looked almost human. "I used to have these," it mused. "Grandma used to give them to me for a special treat."

It put a jelly bean into its mouth and chewed it thoughtfully. Then all of a sudden it spat it out and began to choke and cough, swearing furiously as it did so. Tony took the opportunity to hide behind his desk, but the vampire was so shaky after its coughing fit that it collapsed onto the bed and for several minutes did not move. Then it pulled out a large, blood-spotted handkerchief from under its cape, and blew its nose long and hard.

"That could only happen to me," it grumbled. "My mother did warn me."

"Warned you about what?" asked Tony curiously. He felt much more confident from his position behind the desk.

The vampire glanced furiously across at him.

"Vampires have very sensitive stomachs, stupid. Candy is like poison for us."

Tony felt sorry for him. "Would you like some apple juice instead?" he asked.

The vampire gave a blood-curdling cry. "What are you trying to do? Make me sick?" he yelled.

"I'm sorry," said Tony apologetically. "I was only trying to help."

"That's all right." Apparently the vampire had not taken offense. In fact, thought Tony, it's a very nice vampire, in spite of its looks. Tony had always imagined vampires to be much worse.

"Are you old?" he asked.

"As old as the hills," came the reply.

"But you're much smaller than me."

"So? I was just a kid when I died."

"Oh, I see." Tony had not thought of that. "And are you still . . . I mean, do you have a tomb?"

The vampire grinned. "You could come and visit me if you like. But only after dark. We sleep during the daytime."

"I know," said Tony. At last, here was an opportunity to show off how much he knew about vampires. "If vampires come into contact with sunlight, they die. So they have to hurry through their night's business in order to be back in their tombs by sunrise."

"What a smart kid," sneered the vampire maliciously.

"And if you discover the grave of a vampire," continued Tony, warming to his account, "you have to drive a wooden stake through its heart."

It would have been better not to have said this, because the vampire let out a chilling growl and sprang at Tony. But Tony was too quick. He leaped from under the desk and made for the door with the enraged vampire hard on his heels. Just before he reached the door, the vampire caught him. This is it, thought Tony. He's going to bite. But the vampire just stood panting in front of him, its eyes glowing like hot embers and gnashing its teeth—click-clack, click-clack. It took Tony by the shoulders and shook him. "If you *ever* again even mention wooden stakes, it'll be curtains for you! Understand?"

"Y-yes," stammered Tony. "I-I really didn't mean to upset you."

"Sit down!" barked the vampire. Tony obeyed. The vampire began to pace up and down the room.

"What am I going to do with you now?" it asked.

"We could listen to records," suggested Tony.

"No!" shouted the vampire.

"Or play dungeons and dragons?"

"No!"

"Or I could show you my postcard collection?"

"No, no, *no*!"

"Well, I don't know what we can do then," said Tony, giving up.

The vampire had paused in front of the poster of King Kong, and suddenly it gave a wild cry. "Not that ape!" it yelled, and ripped the poster off the wall, tearing it into shreds.

"That's not very polite," protested Tony. "That was my favorite poster."

"So what?" hissed the vampire. By now, it had discovered all the King Kong books on Tony's bookshelf, and page after page fluttered down onto Tony's bed.

"My books!" howled Tony. "I bought them all with my allowance!"

Suddenly the vampire paused, a happy smile on its lips. "Dracula," it breathed. "My favorite book." It looked at Tony with shining eyes. "Can I borrow it?"

"Sure. But promise to bring it back, okay?"

"Of course." It stuck the book contentedly beneath its cape. "By the way, what's your name?"

"Tony. What's yours?"

"Rudolph."

"Rudolph?" Tony nearly burst out laughing, but luckily stopped himself in time. He didn't want to get the vampire stirred up again. "That's a very nice name," he said. "It fits you."

The vampire seemed flattered. "Tony's a nice name too," he said.

"*I* don't think so," said Tony. "But my father's called Tony too, get it?"

"Oh."

"And my grandfather before him. As if that made any difference to me."

"Up till now I thought Rudolph was a pretty stupid name," said the vampire, "but you get used to it."

"Uh-huh, you get used to it," Tony said, sighing.

"Hey, are you all by yourself like this at home a lot?" the vampire asked.

"Every Saturday."

"Don't you get scared?"

"Sure. Sometimes."

"Me, too," agreed the vampire. "Especially in the dark. My father always says: 'Rudolph, you're not a real vampire. You're a coward.' "

They both laughed. "Is your dad a vampire too?" asked Tony.

"Of course," said the vampire. "What did you think?"

"Your mom, also?"

"Yes. And my sister and my brother and my grandma and grandpa and my aunt and uncle . . ."

"My family is boring and normal," said Tony sadly. "My dad works at the office and my mom's a teacher. I haven't got any brothers or sisters. It's all really boring."

The vampire looked at him sympathetically. "There's always something happening with us."

"Like what? Oh, please tell me!" At last here was a chance to hear a real vampire story.

"Well," began the vampire, "last winter, for instance. You remember how cold it was? When we woke up one day, the sun had already set. I was starving hungry, but when I tried to open the lid of my coffin, I couldn't! I banged on it with my fists, I kicked at it with my feet—but it was no good. I could hear all the rest of the family doing the same thing, all around in the vault. And you know what? For two nights we were iced in and couldn't get our coffins open. Finally it began to thaw, and we barely did it with the last of our strength. We almost died of starvation. But even that's nothing compared to what happened with the new night watchman at the cemetery. Want to hear about that, too?"

"Sure."

"Well, it was on a . . ." began the vampire, but suddenly he broke off. "Can you hear anything?" he whispered.

"Yes," said Tony. A car drew up and stopped. Its doors slammed. "My parents!" cried Tony.

With a leap, the vampire was on the windowsill. "My book?" called Tony. "When . . . ?"

But the vampire had already spread his cape and was gliding away, a dark shadow before the pale crescent of the moon.

Quickly Tony closed the curtains and crept into bed. He heard the front door of the apartment open and his father say: "You see, Hilary? Everything's quiet." Seconds later he was fast asleep.

2 / Parents Know Best

"What do you think about vampires?" asked Tony as he sat at the breakfast table and smeared jelly on his toast. Although he looked as if he was only interested in his toast, in fact he was watching his parents' faces very carefully. First they exchanged surprised glances, and then they began to smile. They're not taking me seriously, thought Tony. They think I'm just being childish. If they only knew.

"Vampires?" asked his mother, hiding a smile. "What in the world made you think of them?"

"Well," said Tony, "they used to exist in the olden days."

"In the olden days," mimicked his father, "people used to believe in the weirdest things. Witches, for instance."

"Witches," Tony scoffed.

"And dwarfs, and ghosts, and fairies . . ." added his mother.

"Haven't you forgotten Santa Claus?" said Tony furiously, and stirred his hot chocolate so violently that it slopped out of his mug and onto the tablecloth. "But I'll tell *you* something: vampires are a totally different ball game."

"Really?" asked his father sarcastically.

"Yes," returned Tony. "And anyone who thinks that vampires only exist in books—" ("Or at Halloween parties," added his mother, giggling) "—is either deaf and blind," continued Tony in a slightly

louder voice, then paused and finished on a soft, mysterious note, "or very, very stupid."

"Oh, dear, you're making me terribly nervous," his mother said, laughing.

"It does seem strange that you and I have never seen one, dear, doesn't it?" his father said to her.

"Aha!" said Tony with satisfaction. "That might happen sooner than you think."

"Help!" said his mother, pretending to be scared.

"You'll see," said Tony, and crammed the rest of his toast into his mouth.

"All I can see is that my cup is empty," said his mother, and smiled. "Pour me out some more coffee, would you, dear?"

Tony's father picked up the coffeepot, and as he poured, he winked at his wife.

Just let them laugh, thought Tony. He leaned back contentedly in his chair and thought of the coming Saturday.

3 / The Giveaway

The following Saturday began the same as usual. After breakfast Dad went shopping. Mom had finished washing her hair and was now busy setting up her old, broken-down hair dryer. Tony was giving her a hand with it.

"Are you going to a movie again tonight?" he asked, trying not to sound too interested in the answer, as he plugged in the cord behind the sofa.

"Maybe," replied his mother. "But there's a chance Dad might have to go to the office instead." She put the hood over her head. "But I might go to the movies anyway, even if he can't come."

"Yeah, why don't you?" encouraged Tony. His heart had sunk at the thought that his mother might stay at home that evening, because, of course, he was expecting a visitor. Meanwhile, his mother had switched on the hair dryer, and under cover of the noise, Tony made his escape to his room, where he had already been getting ready for his guest. Any book that might have upset the vampire had disappeared from his bookshelf, like the last two King Kong books, the one about Tarzan, and the Superman stories. In their place were two new titles: One had a black cover with a picture of a giant-sized bat on it, and in luminous red letters the words: *Twelve Chilling Vampire Tales*. The other had a purple jacket and was called *The Revenge of Dracula*. Tony had deliberately put them where the vampire could not miss them. On the closet hung a picture that Tony himself had painted the evening before. It was a vampire rising from its tomb. Tony was proud of the deathly pale face with black, lidless eyes and a red, gaping mouth, from which protruded teeth as sharp as needles. His mother's reaction on seeing the picture had been encouraging. "Ugh!" she had cried. "Do you have to paint such disgusting things?"

"What do you mean, disgusting?" Tony had answered, carefully touching up the teeth with white paint, so that they seemed to gleam even more brightly.

"Just look at its face. It'd give me nightmares."

But Tony was thinking about the vampire. It would definitely like it.

Now he studied his masterpiece with satisfaction.

The hump of the graveyard in the background, with its tombstones and crosses, added the final gruesome touch. He wondered whether he should put in a couple of bats, but they were hard to draw.

Instead he settled himself on his bed to read. He had already started the first vampire story the day before. It was about a fancy costume party, at which the guests appeared in every kind of costume. One had come as a vampire. His disguise was so good that everyone had been afraid of him; and when midnight struck and everyone removed their masks, he stayed as he was . . . and suddenly everyone realized that he hadn't been wearing a mask at all.

While Tony was reading, his father came home, the telephone rang twice, the vacuum cleaner hummed, water ran in the bathroom—but none of this disturbed him. It wasn't until a piercing cry of pain broke out that he looked up from his story and listened. Had it come from their apartment?

"My foot!" he heard his mother sob.

"Why did you climb onto that rickety chair?" asked his father. "That's why we have a stepladder."

"I know, I know," grumbled his mother, "but it's a little late to think of that."

"Try to stand up."

"Ow!"

"Can you move it?"

"No!"

"What's the matter, Mom?" called Tony.

"I've twisted my ankle," replied his mother.

"Badly?" asked Tony.

"Yes. I'm going to sit with my foot up."

Tony heard her hobble across the hall into the living room, and as he put the book back on the bookshelf, he wondered whether she would be able to drive to the movies that evening with a sprained ankle. He thought she might, as long as it was her left foot, because she didn't have to press the accelerator or brake with that foot. . . . But to Tony's dismay, it was her right foot that was resting on the stool, and she was examining it gingerly.

"What bad luck," she was saying. "It's going to swell up."

"You could put a cold compress on it," suggested Tony.

"Good idea," said Dad.

"Should I run to the drugstore?" asked Tony.

"That would be nice of you, dear," said his mother.

"Oh yeah?" growled his father. "I can think of times when you—"

"Oh, stop bickering, you two," interrupted Mom, and said to Tony, "Be good and ask them what the best thing is for sprains."

And so it happened that Tony spent the afternoon wrapping cold bandages soaked in vinegar around his mother's ankle. His father had gone off to the office a long time ago, and Tony asked for the tenth time: "Tell me the truth, doesn't that feel better?"

"I might begin to think you wanted me out of the house this evening," hinted his mother.

"Oh? Why?" asked Tony, trying to sound hurt.

"Well, you don't have to worry about Dad," she said, smiling. "He's safely in the office. But you didn't figure I'd have an accident, and now you're doing your best to get me up and around again."

"Oh, Mom," Tony said reproachfully, but he didn't sound very convincing.

"Anyway, I've decided to stay at home tonight," she went on. Tony felt the color drain from his face. "And guess what? We'll have a wonderful evening together, just the two of us." Tony could not reply.

"Hey, Tony! What's wrong?" asked his mother.

"N-nothing," he stammered.

"We'll make some popcorn and play Monopoly. It'll be a lot of fun," Mom continued enthusiastically. "Or we could watch television, if you want. Is that why you're looking so worried? Did you think I wouldn't let you watch it?"

"No," he said quietly.

"What's up then?"

"Nothing," he murmured, and looked out of the window. It was already getting dark. "I think I'll go to my room. I feel like reading."

Now *everything* was ruined! If only there were some way of warning the vampire. But how could he let him know? Tony threw himself down on the bed and buried his head in the pillow. He felt lost, helpless, and bitterly disappointed. He had been looking forward to this night for a whole week. Suddenly something knocked at the window—at first so softly that Tony thought he must have imagined it. But then it came again, and Tony sprang from his bed, ran to the window, and tore the curtains open: there on the windowsill sat the little vampire! He smiled, and signaled to Tony to let him in. A quick glance over his shoulder reassured Tony that his bedroom door was shut, and with trembling hands and beating heart, he turned the lock and opened the window.

"Hello," said the vampire. "It's good to see you."

"Ssh!" whispered Tony. "There's an enemy in camp."

"Oh?" said the vampire.

"My mom," whispered Tony. "She hurt her ankle."

This did not seem to worry the vampire. On the contrary, he looked over to the door and licked his lips.

"You wouldn't d-dare . . ." stuttered Tony. The suspicion that had just entered his head was so awful that he did not dare say it out loud.

But the vampire understood very well. He looked slightly embarrassed and said, "No, no, don't worry.

In any case, I just ate." He broke into a grating laugh, which made Tony wince. At that moment the vampire noticed the books. "*Twelve Chilling Vampire Tales*," he read, and sounding pleasantly surprised, he asked, "New?"

Tony nodded. "That one too—*The Revenge of Dracula*."

"*Revenge of Dracula?*" Almost lovingly, the vampire picked up the book. "That sounds incredible."

"Did you bring the other one back?"

"Ahem," coughed the vampire, ashamed. "My little sister has it right now. You'll get it back soon. She begged and begged, and I couldn't say no." Putting *The Revenge of Dracula* quickly under his cape, he said, "I'll return both of them next week."

"Okay," said Tony. "What do you think of my poster?" He pointed proudly to the picture on the closet.

"You did that?" The vampire smiled wryly. "Not bad!"

"What do you think of the vampire?"

"Very good—except the mouth is a little too red maybe."

"Too red? But yours is just as red!"

"Yes," said the vampire, and gave a little cough. "But I have just, er, eaten."

"Oh." Tony sounded taken aback. "I hadn't realized that. Well, I can easily paint over it."

Suddenly he heard the living room door open. "Mom!" he gasped. "Quick! Into the closet."

"Why?" asked the vampire, making for the window. "I can go—"

"No! She'll only stay a second," said Tony. There was a knock on his bedroom door.

"Tony?" called his mother. "Should we make popcorn?"

"Er, um," said Tony, trying hard to think of some excuse. "I'm not hungry yet." He opened the door a crack.

"What about a game of Monopoly then?"

"Maybe later. My book's at a very exciting part."

"Hey, Tony!" said his mother anxiously, trying to look past him into the room. "Are you feeling okay? Is anything the matter?"

"No. Why?"

"There's such an odd smell in here. Tony, have you been playing with matches?" she asked.

"Me? Of course not." Tony sounded hurt.

"There's something fishy going on here," declared his mother, and pushing Tony aside, she marched with determination into the room. She looked around suspiciously, but could not see anything obviously wrong. Then suddenly her eye fell on the closet, and with a cry of "Aha! Then what's this?" she seized a mysterious piece of black cloth, which was sticking out from under the closet door.

"Ow!" came a muffled squeak from the closet. "My cape."

Tony turned white as a sheet. "That's a friend of mine," he said quickly, and moved protectively in front of the closet.

"*Why* is he in the closet?" asked his mother.

"Because . . . he's afraid of the light."

"Well, well, afraid of the light," repeated his mother, unconvinced. "I'd still like to meet him."

"No. I'm sorry, that's impossible."

"Why?"

"Because he's wearing his costume."

"His costume?" His mother sounded amused. "Well, never mind. That's no reason for me not to meet him. Why don't you ask him to have popcorn with us?"

Tony shook his head. "I'm sure he won't want to. He doesn't like popcorn."

"No? Well, what does he like?"

A soft titter was just audible from the depths of the closet.

"Maybe he'd like some soda?" suggested Tony's mother.

"Only if it's red soda!" cackled the voice from the closet.

Tony's mother was slightly perturbed. "We haven't got any cherry soda," she said. "Only cola and root beer."

"Yuk! I *hate* cola and root beer!" spat the vampire.

"Okay. Nothing then," retorted Tony's mother, sounding offended. "I'll go and make the popcorn." And with that she stalked out of the room. She had hardly left before the vampire opened the closet door and scrambled out. He looked even paler than usual and was short of breath.

"What are we going to do now?" asked Tony, pacing up and down with agitation.

"I must fly!" declared the vampire in sepulchral tones.

"You can't just leave me in the lurch! What'll I tell Mom when she asks where you've gone?"

"Oh, just say . . ." began the vampire, but at that moment they heard Mom's approaching footsteps.

"Are you two coming?" she called.

Without further hesitation, the vampire sprang out of the window into the night and was gone.

"Where's your friend?" asked Tony's mother in surprise.

"He—ahem—well, he's gone to the costume party."

His mother looked at him doubtfully. "Funny friends you've got," she said.

"What do you mean, friends?" Tony rose to the attack. "That's only one."

"One like that's more than enough!" his mother said. "I hope I get to really meet him next time.

Anyhow, how did he get out of the apartment?"

"Oh, he was very quiet about it," said Tony. Rats, he thought, now she'll ask me how he got in without ringing the bell, and then what'll I say? But luckily the end of the popcorn maker's popping in the kitchen diverted his mother's attention.

"Snack's ready," she said. "Are you coming?" Tony nodded. "Good. Don't forget to close your window. Otherwise moths will get into your room."

"Or vampires!" added Tony, but his mother didn't hear. Sadly Tony went over to the window. So that was Saturday over, the Saturday he'd been looking forward to so much. Oh, well, maybe next week would be better. He shut the window and closed the curtains.

While they were eating the popcorn, his mother asked, "What was your friend's costume like, exactly?"

"Well, he was dressed as a . . . um. . ." Should he tell his mother? She'd never believe him. "Well, he was going as a vampire."

"A vampire?" echoed his mother. "I wish I had seen him."

"He'll probably wear it when he comes next time," said Tony comfortingly. Then, with a touch of daring, he added: "He wears it almost all the time."

But his mother did not believe him. She just laughed and said, "Tony, you read too many horror stories. You'll be telling me next that he flew out of the window."

"If only you knew," grumbled Tony. Why is it that grown-ups always think they're so smart?

"Oh, Tony, let's not fight about vampires," said his mother soothingly. "Come on, what about that game of Monopoly?"

"Okay," Tony said, sighing. He hadn't thought he *was* arguing about them. He set out the board and gave the dice to his mother. "You start."

"Why me?" asked his mother.

"Oh—got to give you a chance to win *something*."

4 / A Second Cape

"Well, Tony, is that funny friend of yours coming to-night?" asked Tony's mother the following Saturday. She and Tony's father were going to the theater this time, and had put on their best clothes: Mom had on a chiffon dress and a pearl necklace, and Dad was wearing a tailored suit and silk tie. Tony was ready to wave them off at the door. He coughed in slight embarrassment at the question, and answered, "Ahem, well, maybe, if he's not already going to a costume party."

"What?" asked Dad. "Who's going to a costume party?"

"Tony's new friend," answered Mom with a smile. "He's always going to costume parties." Dad looked nonplussed. "And guess what he goes as?" said Mom, laughing. "A vampire." At this Dad looked so puzzled that Tony nearly burst out laughing, but he checked himself. There would only be an argument, and then Dad might stay home out of spite. You could never tell what grown-ups might do.

"Anyway," said Mom, "we'd like to meet this friend *one* day. And his parents, too, of course."

"His parents?" This was *too* much.

"Of course. We want to know what sort of family you're mixing with."

"But I'm not mixing with his family," protested Tony. "Just him."

"That's not the point. Where do they live, as a matter of fact?"

"Come on," interrupted Dad. "We've got to go, Hilary."

"Yes, yes, in a minute. Well, Tony?"

Tony had been hoping that he wouldn't have to answer this one. "Um, n-near the cemetery."

"Where?" His mother was horrified, but Dad took her firmly by the arm and drew her downstairs.

"Don't let your imagination run wild, son," he said. "Costume parties all the time, vampires, cemeteries . . . what next?" He turned and waved.

" 'Bye, dear." His mother waved, too, but looked a little worried. Tony hoped her suspicions had not been aroused.

He shut the door and went back to his room. From his window he watched his parents get into the car and drive away. He hoped Rudolph would be there soon. The sun had set, and the moon was rising high and luminous in the night sky.

Six floors below him, at street level, the lamps were already lit up. A large black moth was fluttering down there, but it began to circle and climb steadily until it was level with Tony's window. A strange transformation began to take place: first, two feet appeared below the wings, then two hands, and finally the familiar, spine-chilling face. It was the little vampire. He did an agile spin in midair and came to land on the windowsill.

"God, you scared me," spluttered Tony.

"Don't say *God*!" The vampire shook himself.

"Do you always fly around looking like a moth?" asked Tony.

"I beg your pardon?" retorted the vampire. "That wasn't a moth. That was a bat."

"Oh," said Tony, embarrassed. He always seemed to say the wrong thing. But the vampire was not really angry. It isn't easy for vampires to smile and look friendly, but Rudolph did his best.

"Are you by yourself?" he asked. Tony nodded. "Good. I've brought something for you," he added, and pulled out from under his cape a second one, just like his own. Tony had only to notice with a shudder the bloodstains and the smell of damp earth and moldy wood that came from it to realize that this was no fake.

"Try it on," whispered the vampire.

"Okay," said Tony doubtfully. He remembered the story of the costume party. Would *he* change into a vampire if he put this thing on? But in the stories he had read, the victim also had to be bitten by a vampire for that to happen. But how did he know what this vampire had in mind? He shuddered suddenly and backed toward the door, knees knocking.

"Hey, Tony." The vampire sounded hurt. "We're friends, remember?"

"Y-yes," stammered Tony, and in his confusion he tripped over his knapsack and fell flat on the floor.

The vampire helped him up. "Do you really think I'd do anything to you?" he asked, looking at Tony steadily.

"N-no," said Tony, blushing. "It's just . . . well, maybe the cape might . . . but it's all crazy!" he added bravely.

"Come on," encouraged the vampire. He picked the cape up off the floor and held it out to Tony. "Put it on."

For a second Tony thought he might throw up, but he gritted his teeth and pulled it over his head. The vampire watched him with glowing eyes.

"Now you can fly."

"Fly? Me?" asked Tony.

"Nothing easier!" The vampire laughed and jumped onto Tony's desk, spreading his arms wide. "Just imagine your arms are wings. Move them up and down, slowly and steadily. Up, down, up, down . . ." He had hardly moved them once before he was gliding around the room. "See?" he said gleefully, landing on the bed. "Now you do it."

With unsteady legs Tony jumped onto the desk and stretched out his arms.

"Now—fly," ordered the vampire.

"I can't."

"Yes. Just believe that you can."

"Can't!"

"Can."

"Oh, all right." Suddenly Tony didn't care if he fell on his head on the floor—he'd show the vampire who was right. The vampire was being totally, completely, ridiculous. Humans just can't fly. So he flapped his arms and jumped and—flew! The air *was* supporting him. It was like swimming underwater—only much, much better.

"I *can* fly," he shouted.

"Of course," growled the vampire. "Now, come with me." He was already sitting on the windowsill and looked around at Tony impatiently. "We've got a lot to do tonight!" He stood up and took off into the darkness.

Tony's fear suddenly seemed to melt away, and without a moment's hesitation, he climbed onto the windowsill, and took a flying leap into the night, following right on the heels of his friend.

5 / Goings-on at the Graveyard

"Where are we going?" asked Tony as they flew along.

"To get the books," replied Rudolph.

"And where—I mean, where exactly are they?"

The vampire grinned. "In my coffin, of course. Where else?"

"Oh!" said Tony, gulping. "So we're going to the cemetery?"

"Yep. Scared?"

"Me? NO!"

"Don't need to be," reassured the vampire. "My family will all be out and about." Tony gave a sigh of relief. The wall of the cemetery was already coming into view. "Ssh!" hissed the vampire, and caught Tony's sleeve. "We have to be careful."

"Why?" asked Tony, but the vampire did not

answer. He seemed to be listening for something.

"Is someone there?" asked Tony anxiously. He guessed they must be somewhere on the far side of the cemetery. Last summer the wall around it had been painted white, but here the stones were gray and crumbling, and moss was growing over them in places. "Is it one of your—relatives?" he asked.

The vampire shook his head. "The night watchman doing his rounds," he hissed. "Come on, let's land."

They had just hidden themselves behind the wall when they heard a loud wheezing. "That's him," whispered Rudolph. He looked worried. "He's looking for us, you know."

"Us?" cried Tony. He was frightened too now.

"Ssh! Us vampires, of course."

"Why?"

"Because he can't stand us. What do you think he carries around in his pocket? A hammer and a wooden stake!"

"How do you know?"

"How do I know?" The vampire grew paler. "Because he drove a wooden stake through the heart of my poor old uncle Theodore."

"Ugh!" exclaimed Tony.

"And all because Uncle Theo wasn't very careful one night, and was sitting on his tombstone just after dusk playing cards. The night watchman just marked which grave it was, and the next day, when it was light . . ." He paused and listened again. All was quiet. "And ever since, he hasn't left us in peace."

"Couldn't you just . . . ?" suggested Tony, and he snapped his teeth to indicate what he had in mind.

"Not him! He chews garlic from dawn to dusk."

"Yuk!" exclaimed Tony. "Garlic."

"I wish he was like the old night watchman," sighed Rudolph. "*He* didn't believe in us, and besides, he had a bad leg. He never used to come into this part of the cemetery, so we practically forgot that there *was* a night watchman." He looked up at the sky thoughtfully. "What a nice man!"

"But the new one does believe in vampires?" asked Tony.

"Unfortunately, yes," answered the vampire. "And that's not all: he's determined to be the first night watchman in America to have a vampire-free cemetery." He looked so upset that Tony felt sorry for him.

"Can't you do anything about him?" he asked.

"Like what?"

"You could move somewhere else."

"Where? Who wants to have eight vampires roosting with them?"

"Hmm," said Tony, and thought about that. "What if you split up? I mean, if one of you went to one cemetery, and one to . . . ?"

But the vampire shook his head decisively. "Out of the question. We vampires stick together!" He stood up and peered over the wall. "He's gone. Now I can show you my coffin."

Tony felt slightly uneasy when they climbed over the wall and suddenly found themselves in the middle of overturned gravestones, crumbing crosses, and thickly growing weeds. There was a deathly hush and quiet, and the graveyard looked creepy in the moonlight. Tony couldn't see anything that looked like a grave in use. The vampire smiled. "It's well hidden, isn't it? You're almost standing on the family vault, and still you don't know where it is."

"Vault?" Tony was surprised. "I thought you each had your own grave."

"A precautionary measure," answered the vampire. "We put all the coffins together in one underground vault, and there is only one entrance, which is well hidden—except of course, there's an emergency exit."

He looked carefully around. Then he picked up a flat stone, overgrown with moss, which lay almost entirely invisible under the shadow of an oak tree. A narrow shaft leading underground was revealed.

"The entrance," whispered Rudolph. "I'll go first, then you follow. But don't forget to put the stone back after you."

Feet first, the vampire slid down the shaft and under the ground.

6 / In the Vault

Tony hesitated for a moment. Should he really follow Rudolph into the vault? How could he be sure it would be all right? But on the other hand, the vampire had never tricked him before, and it was probably much more dangerous to be left alone out here in the cemetery at night. What if one of the other vampires came back? No way! It was definitely better to trust Rudolph, who knew all the dangers in the cemetery, and to climb in after him.

Tony put his legs into the opening and let himself down slowly. At first it seemed sort of exciting to be sliding down into the earth like this, but when it came to actually letting go with his hands, his nervousness once more got the better of him. What would happen if there were a long drop beneath him? Would he ever get out of this hole again? Then he heard

Rudolph's voice close to him saying, "Come on, Tony. Jump!" and he let go with his hands.

He landed on a platform. Above him, just out of reach, he could see the hole he had just come in by. He stood on tiptoe and pushed the stone over the gap. At first he could see nothing in the darkness that enveloped him, and it took a while before his eyes could make out the steps leading down into the inner chamber of the vault. There was only a feeble glimmer of light, and everything smelled of dankness and decay.

"Are you there?" Tony called out anxiously.

"Yes, come on," came the answer.

Cautiously, step by step, Tony made his way downward, and found himself in an inner chamber. It was a low-ceilinged room, which was only half-illuminated by the slender candle burning in a niche near the entrance. Except for the coffins around the walls, it was completely empty. The little vampire was standing on the nearest coffin, a beaming smile on his face.

"Welcome to the Sackville-Bagg vault," he cried, and then added proudly, "Well, what do you think of it?"

"I . . ." began Tony, and hesitated. How could he say that he thought it was one of the most hideous places he had ever been in, and he thought the smell might make him throw up any second?

"Not bad, eh?"

"Why is it called the Sackville-Bagg vault?" Tony asked, changing the subject.

"Because it's the last resting place of the Sackville-Bagg family, of course!" explained Rudolph.

"Is your name Sackville-Bagg too?" asked Tony.

"Yes! Rudolph Sackville-Bagg, if I may introduce myself!"

He made a funny little bow, and Tony noticed how thin and wrinkly his neck was. "And now," continued Rudolph, springing down from his perch, "I'll show you around the coffins!"

He picked up the candle, took Tony by the arm, and went with him right into the vault. The flickering light of the candle threw ghostly dancing shadows on the walls. Tony's throat tightened up with suspense.

"Here you see my dear grandmother's coffin," announced Rudolph, pausing in front of a large coffin that was decorated with many wood carvings. "Sabina the Sinister Sackville-Bagg."

"Why was she sinister?" asked Tony.

"Well, she was just called that in the old days," replied Rudolph. "She was the first vampire in the family, and had to make a name for herself."

Tony looked at the coffin and shuddered. Just think what lay in it during the daytime.

"And this one," went on the vampire by the next

coffin, "is William, my grandfather. Sabina of course bit him first, and so he quickly joined her and was a real help to her on her nightly raids. In those days he was known as William the Wild," he added, chuckling.

"Did he have to, er, make a name for himself too?" asked Tony.

"No, not exactly. But he was renowned for his appetite," answered Rudolph.

Tony felt as though a cold hand were running down his spine. "Whose is that?" he asked hurriedly, moving on to the third coffin.

"That's my father's," replied Rudolph. "Frederick the Frightful Sackville-Bagg, the eldest son of Sabina and William Sackville-Bagg. Next to him is my mother, Thelma the Thirsty. My father was already a vampire when he married her, although my mother never knew anything about it. It was only when he brought her home to the family castle that . . ." He did not finish, just grinned and smacked his lips. "And that," he continued, "is my coffin. You can get in if you like."

"No, thanks," murmured Tony. "I'd rather not."

"Why not?" cried the vampire, and opened up the lid. The inside was lined with black silk, which looked a bit worn-out in places. At the head there was a small black cushion, on which, Tony noticed, lay his two books.

"Is that all?" he asked, somewhat disappointed.

"What did you expect?" asked the vampire.

"Oh, I don't know," said Tony. "I thought coffins were more comfortable."

"Comfortable?" The vampire sounded surprised. "What do you mean?"

Tony realized he'd said something wrong again. "Well, more roomy," he hedged.

"Roomy?" cried Rudolph with feeling. "There's plenty of room. There'd even be room for you in here with me." He got in and lay down, pushing the books to one side. "See? Plenty of room for both of us."

"Yes, I see now. But still, I don't think . . ."

"Stop thinking, then, and just get in here," said the vampire impatiently.

"Ah . . . er," said Tony, quickly going on to the next coffin, "I've been dying to know who this sweet little one here belongs to."

The vampire peered out of his coffin. "My little sister," he said. "But come on in here."

"And what about this one behind here?" continued Tony, ignoring him. *Nothing* was going to get him into a coffin at the same time as a vampire.

"That's my brother's, Gruesome Gregory Sackville-Bagg," said Rudolph, grinding his teeth.

"What's your sister called?" asked Tony, trying hard to divert the vampire. But at that moment, he heard a soft knocking sound that seemed to come out

46

of one of the coffins. He stood stock-still with fright. Were they not alone in the vault after all? Had Rudolph tricked him? But the vampire looked just as surprised and horrified as he did.

"Ssh!" he whispered, climbing nimbly out of his coffin. "That doesn't bode well for us. You must hide!"

"Hide?" cried Tony. "Where can I?"

The vampire pointed to the coffin, whose lid still stood open.

The knocking noise came a second time, but now it was louder and stronger, and they could recognize clearly which coffin it was coming from. "Aunt Dorothy!" gulped Rudolph, sounding really frightened now. His face had paled even more than usual, and his teeth were chattering as though he had frostbite.

"Quick, you have to get in my coffin," he whispered. "If Aunt Dorothy finds you here, you're doomed." Tony didn't have the strength left to argue, and let himself be led to the coffin and helped in.

"And no complaining," warned the vampire sternly before he shut the lid. Then Tony was alone. Darkness as black as pitch enveloped him, and the smell almost made him sick. He could hear Rudolph's voice outside in the vault: "I'm coming right away, Aunt Dorothy." A coffin lid creaked open, and then a deafening argument broke loose.

"What manners!" shrieked a shrill, high voice. "Leaving me here in my coffin to starve. Another ten minutes and I would have starved to death."

"But Aunt Dorothy," said Rudolph, trying to calm her, "why didn't you open the lid yourself?"

"Why?" she scolded. "Because I am so weak and exhausted that I could only knock. A minute more and I would have passed out with hunger!"

From the heaving and groanings that now followed, Tony guessed that Aunt Dorothy was getting out of her coffin. "Oh, I'm so weak and feeble," she moaned. "If only there were something to eat!" But suddenly her voice altered to a low hiss. "What's this?" she cried. "I smell humans."

Tony's heart nearly stopped beating. What if she found him in here?

"Oh, Auntie," reassured Rudolph. "You must be making a mistake."

"I *never* make mistakes," declared his aunt. "But I suppose it could be coming from outside."

"Maybe it's a man taking his dog for a walk," suggested the vampire helpfully. "In any case, you better hurry up, before he gets away."

"Yes, you're right!" Aunt Dorothy's blood was boiling. "I must be off, before he gets away."

Tony heard her gallop up the steps and push the stone to one side. Then everything was quiet. He held his breath and waited. Had Rudolph gone with her?

But then he heard soft footsteps coming back down the stairs, and then, the coffin lid was opened.

"Hi!" said the little vampire, grinning.

Tony lifted his head cautiously and asked, "Has she gone?"

"Yes. She's chasing that man who's walking his dog."

Tony sat perched on the edge of the coffin. He suddenly felt exhausted.

"Well, you don't look very appetizing!" said the vampire cheerfully.

"I want to go home," said Tony in a small voice.

"Home? Why, the night's only just begun." The vampire sounded surprised. But Tony had made up his mind.

"Oh, okay then," grumbled his friend. "We'll fly back together. But don't forget your books."

Barely ten minutes later Tony was back in his own bed. He looked across at the window, which he had been sure to shut behind him, and the night looked black and scary outside. Then he closed his eyes, and fell fast asleep.

7 / Rude Awakening

When Tony woke up the next day, the smell of lunch was already creeping around the apartment. Tony sniffed: macaroni and cheese, browned and crispy in the oven. Yum!

He wondered why he had slept so long, but then remembered that it was very late when he had eventually gone to bed, and the events of the night before went spinning through his mind like a movie. He wondered where the cape was. He was sure he'd put it with his other clothes on the chair, but it wasn't there anymore. What if his parents had found it! The thought of *that* made Tony suddenly very wide awake. He could hear the sound of the washing machine, and his heart sank. He jumped out of bed, and ran into the kitchen, where his father was sitting at the table peeling apples.

"Morning, Tony," he greeted him cheerfully.

"Morning," mumbled Tony.

"Still tired?" grinned his father.

"No-o," said Tony, and cast a sidelong glance at the washing machine. It was certainly washing *something*, but the suds made it impossible to recognize what.

"Are you looking for something?" asked his father.

"No, no," said Tony nonchalantly. He went to the refrigerator and poured himself a glass of milk. "What's in the washing machine?" he asked, taking a gulp of milk so that his father wouldn't see how worried he was.

"Why do you want to know?"

"Because . . . I had some things that needed to be washed too," he said quickly. If only his father would turn off the machine for a second, he could find out whether the cape *was* inside, and if necessary, he could sneak it out.

"What needed washing exactly?" asked his father.

"Socks," said Tony firmly. "My white socks."

"Well, well, your white socks," echoed his father, and it was obvious he was laughing about something. "Well, I'm sorry, but they couldn't go in with that load. It's all the dark things."

"All the dark things?" Tony could not help sounding anxious. "Was there anything of mine in there?"

"Yes," said his father unhelpfully.

"Oh." Tony paused. "What of mine?"

"You'd better ask Mom about that."

"Where is she?"

"In the living room. She's sewing."

"Sewing?" Tony was really worried now. A new and equally upsetting thought had just occurred to him as he remembered how many holes there were in the cape. "Is she sewing . . . socks?" he asked hopefully.

"Not even close." His father smiled. "She found an enormous piece of black cloth, full of holes. . . ."

"Holes?" cried Tony. "Oh, no!" and he rushed off into the living room. He couldn't care less now if his father saw how worried he was.

His mother was sitting by the window and was busy trying to pull a long, thick piece of black thread through the eye of a narrow needle. And on her lap lay . . . Rudolph's cape!

"Ugh!" she said as Tony appeared. "This really stinks."

"It—it b-belongs to a friend of mine," stuttered Tony.

"I know," said his mother. "The poor boy. It's such a raggedy old thing. The holes are big enough to stick your fingers through."

"I don't think he wants them sewn up," said Tony.

"Why in the world do you think that?" asked his mother.

"Well, he said so," said Tony.

In the meantime, his mother had finished darning the second hole, and was trying to thread the needle for the third. "I don't believe it," she said confidently. "No one would want to go around in anything as full of holes as this. Maybe he doesn't have anyone to sew them up for him. No, no," she said adamantly, "I'm sure he'll be pleased to have it fixed. What's his name by the way?"

"Rudolph," grumbled Tony. He had already reached the door. What he really felt like doing was howling with rage: it was a conspiracy, and Dad had just been pretending to be innocent. Well, just wait. He'd show them.

"Do you want any breakfast?" called Dad from the kitchen.

"No," said Tony.

"The macaroni and cheese'll be ready in ten minutes."

"Okay," said Tony. He went back to his room and lay down on the bed. What a mean trick to have played on him, stealing his cape and darning it, without even asking him first. And not only that—to have gone on darning it, even when he'd specifically asked her to stop! Tony was angry with himself too for having left it lying around, even though he knew that his parents always looked into his room in the morning to see if he was still asleep.

But maybe it wasn't such a bad thing that his mother was sewing the cape. In fact, if it didn't have so many holes, the vampire would probably be able to fly better in it. Mom was right after all, and he should be thankful for it.

At that moment he heard his mother coming across the hall, so he quickly stood up and began to make his bed. He was just plumping the pillows when she knocked on his door.

"Tony?"

"Yes. You can come in."

"Here," said Mom. "One cape, as good as new!"

"Thanks," muttered Tony. He took the cape from her and put it on a chair.

"I wanted to wash it," his mother went on. "But then it wouldn't have dried for a long time. And Rudolph wants it back soon, doesn't he?"

"Yes, he does," said Tony quickly.

"Why don't you take it over to him today then?"

"Today? Oh, well—" Tony was at a loss for words. "He's—um, sleeping today."

"What?" his mother said, laughing. "Do you know how late it is?"

"Lunch is ready!" called Dad from the kitchen.

"He really is a funny friend, if he sleeps all day," said Mom, giving Tony a searching look. "You've got to tell more about him during lunch."

"Oh. Uh, I'm not very hungry today," said Tony,

even though his stomach was churning in anticipation of the macaroni and cheese.

"Don't be ridiculous!" said Mom, and Dad called, "He hasn't even had breakfast yet."

"Oh, all right," grumbled Tony. In any case, macaroni and cheese was his favorite lunch, although today he didn't really feel like it. He thought worriedly about how it would be at the table, when every mouthful would be punctuated by questions about why Rudolph slept so late.

"Good, isn't it?" said Dad, who was already on his second helping.

"Delicious!" agreed Mom. "Tony doesn't seem to be enjoying it much, though." Tony felt himself turn red. "Tell me," said Mom suddenly. "What's Rudolph's last name?"

Tony's heart stood still. "Why?"

"Why? Because I'm interested, that's all."

"Bagg," muttered Tony.

"What?" Tony's mother could not believe it. "Rudolph Bagg?"

"Sackville-Bagg, really," corrected Tony. "Rudolph Sackville-Bagg."

"That's even worse," said Dad, laughing.

"Tony Noodleman isn't much better," shouted Tony.

"Now, now." Dad grinned. "We're all called Noodleman, young man."

"Yes. But it's all right for you," cried Tony. "You're grown-ups. People don't laugh at you."

"Just be thankful you're not called Noodleman-Bagg," remarked Mom.

But Tony didn't think that was particularly funny. Grumpily he fixed his eyes on his plate. They were always laughing at him.

"Tony," said his mother, "where's your sense of humor?"

"May I be excused?" was all Tony could reply.

"In a minute," said his mother. "What are you going to do about the cape? Will you take it over now?"

"Er—okay," said Tony.

"I could drive you over there," offered Dad.

"Over where?"

"To your friend's house, of course," said Dad. "I'll be going past the cemetery."

"Th-the cemetery?" Tony turned white as a sheet.

"I thought you said he lived near the cemetery?" said his mother.

"Y-yes, he does," murmured Tony.

"Then you can show me where exactly," said Dad.

"And ask him over," added Mom.

"B-but . . ." stuttered Tony helplessly. "He'll still be asleep, and anyway, I feel like taking a walk. . . ."

"My goodness!" exploded his father. "Tony Noodleman feels like taking a walk. This *is* a special occasion."

"Let him then," said his mother, and turning to Tony she added: "But if you go by yourself, I insist you invite him over here. We want to meet him." She paused for a moment. "Ask him for Wednesday. Then I'll be able to make a cake."

"I-I'll be going then." Tony backed away.

"Don't forget the cape," called Mom. "And remember: Wednesday, at four o'clock."

8 / The Heart-shaped Gravestone

Sunday afternoon from lunchtime until four o'clock was the most boring time of the whole week, thought Tony—it always seemed to go so slowly. Up till one o'clock everything smelled deliciously of the Sunday lunch, but that was quickly gobbled up, and then everyone just rested. From that point on, children must preferably not be seen, and certainly not be heard. Playing hockey in the street or zooming around on your bicycle were not worth the risk.

So when Tony took the elevator down to the ground floor, it was not surprising to find it completely empty. The street was dead quiet too. Not a car passed. Tony wandered along, balancing on the curb and swinging the plastic bag with the cape in it. He knew that his parents were standing on the balcony waving to him, but he stared stonily in front of him. They could wave till the cows came home for all he cared. It would teach them if he never came back alive. In fact, he wasn't too sure what exactly he was going to do at the graveyard. How was he ever going to get the cape into the tomb in the daylight? And how was he ever supposed to invite Rudolph over? Should he leave a note? Luckily he had thought of this and had brought a pad of paper and a pencil with him. But he was pretty sure that there was no mailbox at the tomb. And if he went into the vault himself, and left the note on Rudolph's coffin, the other vampires would be sure to wake up, and then what would happen? Tony walked more and more slowly the nearer he got to the cemetery. Finally he came to a standstill. He knitted his brows and stood deep in thought.

"Hi, Tony!" came a voice.

"What are you doing here?" he asked, and blinked. Before him stood Robert, a boy from the seventh grade whose nickname was "Blabbermouth" because he was always talking about things that were none of his business.

"What brings *you* here is more like it," he said, standing with legs apart and arms folded, across Tony's path.

"I'm . . ." Tony tried to be vague. "I'm just going for a walk around here." That was a really dumb answer, he knew, and he realized it would not satisfy

Robert, but he had not been able to think of anything better in time. He wondered if he should have told him the truth, but Robert would never have believed him. If he had, he might have disappeared without any more discussion.

"I'm just going for a walk around here," mimicked Robert with a sneer. "Can't you think of a better reason than that?"

"Yeah," said Tony. "I'm going to visit a friend of mine."

"Anyone I know?" asked Robert with menace in his voice.

"Doubt it," said Tony, smirking, "unless you know any vampires!"

Just for a moment Robert was too taken aback to reply, but then he said scornfully, "Vampires! That's so funny, I forgot to laugh." He shook his head, and then towered menacingly over Tony. "Just beat it. And don't let me see you hanging out around here again!"

"Okay, okay," said Tony. "Don't lose your cool, man." And he went on his way, swinging the bag and whistling. Robert'd better not think that he had frightened him, even if he was two grades ahead of him. He reached the wall of the cemetery without looking back. It was painted white and so high that Tony could only see the tops of the oak trees over it. Just before he reached the gates he stopped and looked furtively around, but Robert had vanished. Tony waited for another minute or two, but when still nothing happened, he opened the gate and slid inside.

The silence of the cemetery stole over him, and he was aware of the smell of earth and flowers. Not so bad after all, thought Tony, and feeling less scared, he walked on. If it had not been for all the crosses and gravestones, with crazy things like *Rest in Peace* engraved on them, he might have thought he was walking through the park. The only odd thing was that he did not see anybody else, but maybe Sunday afternoon wasn't the right time for visiting grave-yards. Never mind, that made things all the better for him—he could be sure of not being disturbed.

He went on down the main pathway. He had been here before with his mother, when she came to visit their relatives' graves. So he already knew that the wilder part of the cemetery began behind the chapel, which was in front of him at the end of the path. He always thought this chapel looked rather cozy; it was built like a normal house, except that it didn't have any windows, only a door made of iron. And although the chapel itself looked old and weathered, at the door hung a brand-new and obviously frequently used padlock, which Tony found totally bizarre, because not once had he seen anyone go in or come out of the place.

Today he crept past the building with an uneasy

feeling in his stomach. Nothing had changed about it; even the padlock gleamed in the afternoon sun. He wondered whether the chapel was empty. And if it wasn't, what was lurking inside? Nothing pleasant, he decided, and was reminded of the story *Night in the Morgue*, which he had read not long before: a man had spent a night in a morgue in order to win a bet, and at first had thought he was alone. But when the moonlight shone in through the window, one of the cabinets had begun to open, and out came . . . Tony felt a cold shudder run down his spine at the thought, even though the sun was shining.

Suddenly he was in a hurry to return the cape and get out of the cemetery. Who knew what might be lurking there? Vampires weren't the only things Tony read about—in fact they were probably the most harmless—what about the bodies that weren't really dead? Tony had once read about a woman who knocked at the lid of her coffin in increasing despair until finally she died of exhaustion.

Tony quickened his steps. If anyone were to start knocking, he, Tony, certainly would not go to investigate! The best thing would be to run so fast that he wouldn't even hear any knocking. He hadn't forgotten old Aunt Dorothy in the vault the night before.

By now Tony had left the part of the cemetery where the paths were raked and the hedges neatly trimmed. Here, behind the chapel, the grass grew knee-high, and he had to make his way through brushwood and weeds. But he could see the wall of the cemetery in the distance. The oak tree must be around here somewhere, and with it, the entrance to the vault. As he went farther, he suddenly thought he could hear steps on the gravel behind him. A cold shiver ran through him. Who or what could be following him? Something that had come out of the chapel?

But the next moment everything was quiet again, and he dared to look around—the cemetery lay as still as before. He must have imagined the footsteps; after all, it was pretty lonely here, and it wasn't surprising to start imagining things.

Tony almost stumbled over a gravestone that lay hidden in the grass. It was an unusual stone, in the form of a heart. And across it in flourishing, barely legible letters was written: "Frederick Sackville-Bagg, 1803–1850." Tony shivered, for if these dates were right, Rudolph's father had already been dead for over a hundred years. A few paces farther on he discovered another stone, also in the shape of a heart, which bore the inscription: "Thelma Sackville-Bagg, 1804–1851," and nearby he found the grandparents' stones: "Sabina Sackville-Bagg, 1781–1847," and "William Sackville-Bagg, 1780–1848." A yard or two farther on lay the gravestone of Great-Aunt Dorothy, and near that, Uncle Theodore. And each one was in the same heart shape. Tony thought it was altogether too much. What on earth was the heart supposed to mean, anyhow? First, love—Tony laughed—and second, blood! Everyone knew that it was the heart that pumped blood through the body.

As Tony compared the dates it occurred to him that the vampires had all died in a particular order, and all within a year of one another: first Sabina, then William, Thelma, Frederick, Dorothy, and Theodore. Did that mean that each one had . . . ? And what about the children? Who had . . . ? Where were their gravestones anyway?

Tony looked and looked, but he could only find ordinary gray stones that certainly were not covering any vampire's grave. Perhaps his friend the vampire and his sister just didn't have any stones. They were probably the last of the Sackville-Baggs to die, and there was no one left to give them a real vampire burial. As he was musing about this, he heard a rustling in the bushes near him, and turning around, he saw the grinning face of Robert.

"You?" was the only thing he could think of to say.

"Surprised?" Robert pushed his way out of the bush with a complacent grin on his face. "Why do you look so scared? Did you think I was a ghost?"

"Er, I," murmured Tony, "I thought it was . . ."

"A monster!" smirked Robert.

"No! I thought it was my friend," explained Tony.

"We arranged to meet here, but he hasn't shown up yet." He wondered if Robert would believe him, but he couldn't think of any better explanation at the moment.

"Oh, yeah? Think I buy that?" said Robert scornfully, and then, grabbing hold of Tony's chin and forcing his eyes up to meet his own, he continued: "You think I'm stupid or something?"

"Ow!" protested Tony, but Robert held it even tighter.

"You watch it," he said menacingly. "Just tell me what's going on here."

"Let go first," demanded Tony.

"Okay," agreed Robert, and took a step backward. "So?"

"I wasn't lying," said Tony. "I really am meeting a friend here."

"And what's this friend called?"

"Rudolph. Rudolph Sackville-Bagg."

Robert's expression became suspicious again. "And what are you both up to in a graveyard?"

Tony's mind worked feverishly. No way could he mention the vault, because Robert would surely blab, and then the whole vampire clan would be lost.

"We, er, we were going to look for vampire graves!" he said finally.

"Vampire graves," scoffed Robert, with a yawn. "Kids' stupid stories."

"No, no," protested Tony. "There are supposed to be vampires in Rudolph's family way back."

"Ha, ha!" said Robert loudly but without sounding amused.

"There's something special about their graves," Tony continued.

That seemed to catch Robert's attention. "Something special?" he echoed.

"Yeah. The gravestones." Tony let his voice sink to a whisper, and he looked furtively around him. "They're in the shape of a heart."

"A heart?" echoed Robert.

"Don't you see?" explained Tony. "Hearts mean blood!"

Robert's lips curved in a scornful smile. "What garbage," he said. "You'd never find even half a gravestone in the shape of a heart."

Tony had to make an effort not to laugh out loud. "We'll see, we'll see," he said. "And anyway, it doesn't hurt to look."

"So why weren't you looking?" asked Robert.

"Because I was waiting for my friend," said Tony patiently.

One thing was good, anyway: he had turned Robert's interest to the gravestones. He could see that Robert *was* intrigued, because he kept shifting from foot to foot.

"Want to bet on it?" said Robert at last. "A dollar

for you if we find the gravestones, and two dollars for me if we don't."

"Why do you get two dollars and me only one?" demanded Tony.

Robert put on his snotty seventh-grade smile. "Because a dollar for you is the same as two for me."

"That's not fair," said Tony. "I'd have to *pay* you two if I lost!"

"Oh, you're going to lose then, are you?" mocked Robert.

"Well," said Tony, unable to conceal a smug smile. "We'll see. . . ."

"So, fine—let's move it!" said Robert. "I'll start here, and you go over there."

Tony had only taken a few steps toward the chapel when he heard Robert cry out, "Tony, come here, quick! I've found them!"

Tony tried to look surprised. "Really?" he said.

Robert was beside himself. "God!" he said again and again. "Gravestones in the shape of hearts! Look at this one: Frederick Sackville-Bagg, 1803–1850, and Thelma Sackville-Bagg, 1804–1851." He looked at Tony with wide eyes. "Hey! Didn't you say your friend was called Sackville-Bagg too?"

Tony tried not to look too pleased. "Yep," he said with a nod.

By now Robert had found the other gravestones, and his voice faltered as he listed the names. "Sabina,

William, and here—Dorothy. What weird names they all had!" The two boys smiled. "But they've all been dead for years," Robert continued. "Or do you think they still fly?"

"I thought you didn't believe in such stupid stories?" teased Tony.

"Well, no, I don't," mumbled Robert. "But this gravestone thing . . ." He paused, then said: "Hey, didn't you say your friend was a vampire too?"

"Did I say that?"

"Sure. Back outside the cemetery."

"Then I guess I meant it," said Tony.

Robert took a step closer to Tony and looked at him warily. "Did you mean it?"

Tony just smiled. "I could tell you many a tale if you believed in vampires."

"Maybe I do believe in them now," said Robert. "And if you don't, you could always introduce me to your friend to convince me."

"Now?" grinned Tony.

"Why not?" answered Robert. He was getting annoyed with Tony's obvious enjoyment and I-know-more-than-you smiles.

"I can't," said Tony calmly, "because vampires don't get up till after sunset, and it's still daytime at the moment."

"So why did you say you'd arranged to meet him then?"

"Well, I had to start this stupid story somewhere, didn't I?"

Robert was so surprised that for a second he just looked at Tony without saying a word. Then he turned bright red, and his voice cracked with anger. "You—you little creep! Just shut up about your vampires! It's all garbage anyway."

"But you believed me," said Tony, laughing.

"I did not!" screamed Robert.

Tony just kept grinning.

"And anyhow," concluded Robert, "I'm going home!" He turned on his heels and stamped off.

Just then an idea occurred to Tony. What if Robert were to come on Wednesday and not Rudolph . . . but not as Robert, as Rudolph . . . that was it! The answer! His parents would stop bothering him, because they would think they had met Rudolph at last.

"Rob-bert!" called Tony as loudly as he could, and ran off after him. "Wait up!"

9 / Anna the Toothless

Tony was already asleep when something tapped gently on his window. Blinking his eyes sleepily, he could only make out through the drawn curtains the outlines of two dark shapes crouching on the windowsill. It had to be vampires, for who else would be outside in the middle of the night, tapping on a window on the sixth floor. But he wondered why there were two. Rudolph always came alone. What if it were a trap! What if Rudolph's family had found out where he, Tony, lived! But Rudolph would definitely have warned him if that had happened. No, Tony decided, it was probably just Rudolph outside—but who in the world had he brought with him?

The tapping came again, this time more impatiently. Tony tiptoed over to the window and peeped through the curtains. He recognized his friend the vampire, with his cape wrapped tightly around him, and by his side a second, much smaller vampire, who was also wearing a black cape.

Tony heard a whisper from outside. "It's me, Rudolph!" His heart beating loudly, Tony pulled the curtains to one side and there sat a girl vampire! He was so surprised that for a second he was speechless, rooted to the spot.

"Open up!" called Rudolph, sliding restlessly backward and forward on the windowsill. Tony quickly opened the window, and the two vampires slipped noiselessly into the room.

"My sister," said Rudolph, indicating the girl vampire. "Anna the Toothless." Her face was small and very white, with pink eyes and a round little mouth. She smiled shyly at Tony, and two red spots appeared on her cheeks as she turned on her brother.

"You shouldn't introduce me as Anna the Toothless," she complained. "First of all, they're growing, and anyway, you didn't have any either when you were my age!"

"She's the only one in our family who drinks milk," said the vampire, and laughed.

"Not anymore!" said Anna defiantly.

"She insisted on meeting you," continued the vampire.

Anna's face turned an even deeper shade of red. "So?" she said, glaring at her brother. "Isn't that allowed?" Turning to Tony, she added: "In fact, I wanted to see your books. He—" and she pointed at her brother "—told me that you had shelves and shelves." She went over to the bookshelf and picked one out. "What about this one? *Twelve Chilling Vampire Tales*. Will you lend it to me?"

"Er, okay," said Tony.

"Thank you," she said, smiling, and tucked the book under her cape, at the same time throwing a triumphant look in the direction of her brother.

She would really look very pretty for a vampire, thought Tony, if only her face weren't so pale, and if she didn't have those dark rings under her eyes . . . but what did it matter? Like he was interested in girl vampires!

Meanwhile, Rudolph had made himself comfortable at Tony's desk and was looking around inquisitively. "By the way," he asked, "where's that other cape of mine?"

Tony had been dreading that question. "Well," he began, noticing out of the corner of one eye that Anna was leafing through one book after another, "it's not here, exactly."

"Not here?" questioned the vampire.

"I lent it to someone."

"*Lent* it?" The vampire looked angry and suspicious. "Why?"

"Um, well, my parents . . ." He trailed off, realizing

for the first time that his parents were asleep in the next room. He continued in a whisper, "My parents wanted me to ask you over."

"Me?" cried the vampire in amazement.

"Yes, you," said Tony, "because I'd told them so much about you. That's why I had to go to the cemetery with the cape today."

"To the cemetery?" repeated the vampire. "Why didn't we see each other?"

Even Anna pricked up her ears. "I didn't see you either," she said.

"It was in the daytime," explained Tony.

"Too bad," sighed Anna.

"Anyway, when I got to the cemetery, this guy from school—" Rudolph didn't have to be told they were friends, after all "—turned up, and suddenly I had a great idea. Robert could pretend to be you!"

"How's he going to do that?" asked Rudolph.

"Well, I'll introduce him as Rudolph Sackville-Bagg."

"Would it work?" asked the vampire nervously.

"Sure. My parents have never met Robert. And anyway, I told him all about it."

"*All* about it?" asked the vampire in a meaningful voice, looking dangerously at Tony.

Tony quickly reassured him. "Of course, nothing about the vault, or about your relatives. Anyway, he doesn't believe in vampires."

"That's lucky," said Rudolph, and breathed a sigh of relief.

"But Tony believes in us!" warbled Anna, and gave a little skip and a jump.

"Cut it out!" hissed the vampire.

Anna looked downcast. "Can't you stop picking on me?" she said. "What will Tony think?"

"I would imagine it's too late to worry about that," teased the vampire. "He must have realized by now that you're just a dumb little baby who thinks he's a hero!"

"Wh-a-at did you say?" screeched Anna, marching furiously over to Rudolph. "If you ever say that again . . ." And she shook her tiny fist in his face.

"Okay, okay," relented Rudolph. "I'm sorry."

Quieted by this, Anna gave Tony a heartfelt look and returned to her place on the bed.

"So when do I get my cape back?" resumed the vampire.

"Y-your cape?" stammered Tony. He was still watching the door anxiously, knowing that it might be flung open at any moment. Usually his parents woke up at the slightest cough. Even quiet music disturbed them, and already Tony had had some explaining to do about his radio. Anna had just that moment discovered it. She was turning the knobs curiously, and before Tony could do anything, raucous rock music blared out across the room.

"Oh, no!" groaned Tony, but too late. The door of his parents' bedroom had opened.

"Quick!" he hissed, and switched off the radio. "Hide!"

Rudolph and Anna hardly had time to crawl under Tony's bed before his mother appeared in the doorway. Her face looked gray and crumpled, and her hair stood out from her head in wild ringlets.

"Tony," she said sleepily, "how often have I told you . . . ?"

"I know, I know," interrupted Tony. "I'm sorry."

His mother gave him one of her reproachful looks and shook her head, then turned as if to go. But then she stopped. "Tony," she said, "there's a funny smell in here."

"I can't smell anything," said Tony innocently.

"I can. Something smells . . . moldy."

"Moldy?" repeated Tony, stationing himself in front of the bed.

"Something smells in here," said his mother emphatically. She went slowly round the room, sniffing suspiciously in each corner. Luckily she didn't look under the bed, but came to a standstill in the middle of the room.

"When was the last time you took a bath, Tony?" she asked.

"Yesterday," said Tony, ignoring the soft giggle that came from under the bed.

"There's nothing to laugh about," said his mother sternly. "You know you should take a bath every day." Sniffing indignantly she added, "You smell as if you need one!" There was another titter from under the bed.

"Okay, laugh!" shouted his mother. "It won't seem so funny in the morning. I'll see to it that you wash, my boy!" With this last remark she stalked out, shutting the door behind her with a determined click. Tony made sure he heard his parents' door close before he sank onto his bed in relief.

"By the skin of our teeth!" he breathed.

"What's that about teeth?" asked Anna, wriggling out from under the bed.

"Just a figure of speech," said Rudolph, "but of course, babies can't be expected to understand."

"Huh!" sniffed Anna, and stuck out her tongue.

"We must be going," announced the vampire.

"Already?" asked Anna sadly.

"Now," growled the vampire, and jumped onto the windowsill. "It'll soon be light. Come on!"

Anna looked pleadingly at Tony. "May I come again?" she asked.

"Er, of course," said Tony, a little confused.

"Great!" she gurgled, and with a single bound was out through the window, looking surprisingly like an oversized butterfly hovering outside.

"What about the cape?" asked the vampire. "When do I get it back?"

"Wednesday," answered Tony.

"Okay," said the vampire, and added softly, "It's just that it's not even mine. I got it out of Uncle Theodore's coffin!"

"The one with the wo . . ." Wooden stake was what Tony had been about to say, but he had stopped himself just in time. He remembered only too well how vampires feel about wooden stakes. But in any case, Rudolph had missed Tony's last words, and had already sailed off into the night.

As long as Robert remembers the cape on Wednesday, everything will be all right, Tony just had time to think before he fell asleep.

10 / Robert's Great Performance

"Your Rudolph isn't the most punctual of friends," said Tony's mother on Wednesday. The clock said four thirty and Robert still had not arrived.

"Never mind," said Tony. "It doesn't matter."

"Of course it matters," contradicted his mother. "This isn't your everyday snack."

Tony thought the table looked as if she was expecting a state visit. All the best china was out, and the silver spoons and even the candlesticks. A special cake had been baked that very afternoon for the occasion, and it smelled delicious; there were Tony's favorite cookies, tea in a fancy pot, and even chocolate milk shakes instead of just the regular old milk.

"Shouldn't you call him up?" suggested his mother, and before Tony could answer, she had pulled out the telephone book. She ran down the list of names with her finger. "Sack, Sackerman, Sackmore, Sack-stone, Sackwood. There isn't a Sackville-Bagg," she said, and looked questioningly at Tony.

"I could have told you that," said Tony.

"Did you know they don't have a phone?" asked his mother.

"Well, I didn't know, but I figured they might not," said Tony.

"Why?" His mother was all ears now. But at that very moment the doorbell rang.

Tony leaped up in relief. "That must be him!" he said, and ran to the door. I hope it really is Robert, he thought. What in the world am I going to say to Mom and Dad if he's left me in the lurch?

But it was Robert. At first Tony could hardly recognize him in his dark pants, black shirt, and wrapped, according to instructions, in the famous cape.

"Hi!" He grinned. "How do I look?"

Tony looked quickly over his shoulder. "Ssh!" he whispered. "We can't give the act away." Out loud he said, "Hi, Rudolph! Come on in."

Mom appeared in the hall. "How nice," she cooed. "Hello, Rudolph. I'm very pleased to meet you."

"Good afternoon," said Robert, making a low bow.

"You know your way around the apartment already," said Tony's mother, watching Robert closely, "but we've never met. Once you hid in the closet, and then when our snack was ready, you disappeared." Robert just stood and grinned. "Anyway," continued Tony's mother, "what do you think of your cape?"

"The cape?" repeated Robert. "It's great."

"Haven't you noticed anything different about it?"

Robert looked puzzled. "What kind of things?"

"The holes, of course," Tony's mother said, laughing. "I've darned them."

"Oh, er, yes—thank you very much," murmured Robert.

"Tony said you didn't want them fixed."

"Really? Why?"

Tony came to the rescue. "Because then it wouldn't look like a real vampire costume," he chipped in.

"Oh, yes." Robert looked totally confused. "My vampire costume. Well, Mrs. Noodleman, it's just that it looks more spooky with holes in it."

Tony's mother smiled. "Come along in," she said. They were over the first hurdle, thought Tony. Robert wasn't bad, he'd give him that. In fact, for the dollar it was going to cost him, the performance was cheap at the price.

"I hope you're enjoying your cake," said Tony's mother when they were all sitting around the table.

"Mmm, thank you," mumbled Robert, who had already devoured a quarter of the whole thing and was now cramming a cookie in his mouth.

"I really didn't know what to make for you," said Tony's mother, smiling. "Tony told me such amazing stories about what you liked to eat." She poured herself a cup of tea. "He said you only ate or drank one thing, and that we didn't have any of it in the house."

"How strange," said Robert.

"But I can see now that you've got a very good appetite," said Tony's mother, looking pleased.

Robert nodded and took another cookie. "I've always liked eating," he said through a mouthful of crumbs. "My mom always says: 'Robert, you'll eat us out of house and home!'"

"What does she call you?" asked Tony's mother, surprised. "Robert?"

"Er, yes, that's my middle name," said Robert quickly. "Rudolph Sackville—" He hesitated, and looked desperately at Tony.

Sackville-Bagg. Tony's lips silently mouthed the name.

"Sackville-Wagg!" said Robert firmly.

Tony's mother was even more confused. "What?" she said.

"I mean Sackville-Bang," Robert tried again.

"Oh, you're just trying to pull my leg."

"No, no, Mrs. Noodleman, of course not," Robert assured her, reaching for another cookie.

"Hey!" yelled Tony. "Leave some for other people!"

"Tony," scolded his mother. "You shouldn't speak
to your guest like that."

"I don't know who's behaving like a guest around
here," stormed Tony. "Guests don't guzzle their way
straight through a quarter of a cake!"

" 'Course they don't," agreed Robert peaceably, cut-
ting himself another piece. "They eat half!"

Tony was speechless. He'd invited Robert over and
now the pig was devouring the cake as if he hadn't
eaten for a week. What in the world was his mother
going to think? "Rudolph, I think it's time you were
going," he said in a strange voice.

Robert did not agree. He grinned unashamedly,

and proceeded to pile his plate with chocolate cookies. "Why should I?"

"Because . . ." began Tony, but he was interrupted by the sound of the door bell.

"That'll be Dad," said Tony's mother, getting up.

"Dad?" asked Tony, sounding surprised.

"He arranged to come home early," explained his mother.

Once she had left the room, Tony turned on Robert. "If you think you can come here and do just what you like . . ." he hissed, but Robert interrupted.

"Now, calm down," Robert said with mock concern.

"I'll . . . I'll . . ." But before he could find the appropriate threat, his father came into the room.

"Hello, Rudolph," he said.

Robert half rose from his chair. "Afternoon."

"So, at last we've got the chance to get to know you," said Tony's father, sitting down. He doesn't even notice me, thought Tony grumpily. But I guess I'm not a guest!

"You're the one who thinks it's always Halloween," said Tony's father conversationally.

"I-I do?" asked Robert.

"Tony's told us that you're always dressed for a Halloween party."

"Ow!" cried Robert as Tony landed a sharp kick on

84

his shin from under the table. "Er, yes, I suppose I am."

"How do you work it in the summer?" pursued Tony's father.

Robert didn't know what to say, so he said nothing and took another cookie instead.

"Do you have a special party?" asked Tony's father, smiling.

"Maybe he doesn't want to talk about it," suggested Tony quickly.

"Exactly." Robert nodded.

Tony's father pointed to the cape and remarked, "You're even wearing your costume today. Are you going to pretend it's Halloween tonight?"

"Not tonight," said Robert. "Tomorrow, probably. Now, I really must be going."

"So soon?" asked Tony's mother, appearing from the kitchen with a fresh pot of tea.

"I'm afraid so," said Robert. "I've got to get some things ready."

"What sort of things?" asked Tony's father. "Do you have to polish your vampire teeth? Or have you got a set of those rubber fangs?"

"Rubber fangs?" Robert was completely lost.

"Yes. All the best vampire costumes have rubber fangs to go with them. If you don't have two pointed teeth, you're not a real vampire!"

Robert had turned pale. He even seemed to have lost his appetite, for he stood up, murmuring, "I've got to go."

"Good-bye," called Tony's parents.

" 'Bye," said Robert.

Tony went with him to the door. When they were out of earshot, he asked, "Why did you get up so suddenly?"

"Why?" sneered Robert. "Because I don't like being cross-examined, that's why. I suddenly realized that I'd met your father."

"No!" gasped Tony. "Where?"

"My dad works in the same office as yours."

"Did he recognize you?" asked Tony.

"I hope not," said Robert. "Look what I look like." He grinned. "See you, Tony."

"Wait!" cried Tony. "The cape!"

"Oh, yeah, this old rag," said Robert, pulling it off. "Here you go; I'm not wearing that again."

Tony quickly rolled it up and stuck it under his sweater. " 'Bye, Rudolph!" he said loudly enough for his parents to hear, and shut the door. Thank goodness that was over. Now all he had to do was hide the cape. He tiptoed across the hall. The door of the living room was open, and he could hear his parents talking quietly. They were probably still at the table discussing Rudolph.

"Tony!" called his mother. "Is that you?"

"Coming, coming," he answered, and slipped into his room.

"What's the matter?" asked his mother.

"Nothing," replied Tony, stuffing the cape under his bed. "Here I am."

As he had guessed, his parents were sitting at the table with puzzled expressions on their faces. "Well?" asked Tony bluntly. "What did you think of him?"

"He wasn't very talkative," said his mother.

"He never is," said Tony.

"And I've met better-behaved boys," she went on.

"So've I," agreed Tony, thinking wistfully of the chocolate cookies.

"In fact, I can't figure out why he's such a good pal of yours," announced his mother.

Me neither, thought Tony. Out loud he asked, "What about you, Dad. What did you think?"

"Well, I didn't see much of him. But I got the feeling I'd seen him somewhere before."

"Mmm." Tony couldn't resist a smile. "I wonder."

"Do you think I have?" asked his father.

"Of course not." Tony had never looked so innocent. He felt pretty good. Everything had gone according to plan. And it was highly unlikely that his father would ever remember where he had met Robert—at least, he hoped not!

11 / At Dusk

"Would you mind if I went to my room?" asked Tony politely.

"Of course not," said his mother. "But why?"

"I've got something to do for school," said Tony. This wasn't exactly true, but it was always a good excuse, and one that his parents never objected to. Once in his room Tony threw himself down on his bed. Robert thought he was so cool, he thought. He was, of course, very grateful that Robert had played the game at all, and what's more, he'd done it very well—his parents hadn't suspected a thing! But all that stuffing himself. Still, at least now his parents knew who Rudolph was, and wouldn't bother him anymore about meeting his friend—after all, they'd had plenty of him that afternoon.

Tony must have fallen asleep, because when he

opened his eyes, it was already getting dark. Everything was quiet in the apartment. Maybe his parents had gone out? Tony went to the door and listened carefully. There wasn't a sound to be heard. If his parents were at home, the television was usually on, or at least the radio, and sometimes they even talked to each other. Tony decided they must have gone out for a walk.

He was thirsty, and suddenly remembered the chocolate milk shake his mother had made for Robert. Maybe there was some left. A search of the refrigerator revealed a piece of the cake, but no milk shake, only orange juice. Tony had to be content with that, and taking the cake with him, he went back to his room. As he crossed the hall he noticed a strange, rather moldy smell, which had not been there before. It was not the cape; that just smelled of old clothes. And it could not be Rudolph, because he always smelled kind of burned. Was it one of the other vampires? After all, he had left his window open. . . .

He opened his bedroom door cautiously and asked: "Is anyone there?" A low chuckle was the only answer.

"Rudolph?" he called into the gloom.

"No!" came the reply, followed by a high-pitched giggle.

"Anna!" guessed Tony.

"Right!" The lamp by Tony's bed was switched on,

and its light revealed Anna sitting on the bed, looking pleased with herself. She looked different: her hair, which on Sunday had hung in wild tangles down to her shoulders, had been brushed till it gleamed. Her eyes shone, and excitement had brought color to her deathly pale cheeks. What in the world was she doing here, wondered Tony. He hoped she was not on the prowl. Anna must have guessed his thoughts, because she began to laugh. "Have you forgotten I'm called Anna the Toothless?" she asked.

Tony felt like an idiot. Unable to think of anything else to say, he held out the glass and asked: "Do you like orange juice?"

She shook her head. "No. But I'd love some milk."

"Wait a second," said Tony, and a moment later he returned with a glass of milk.

"Thanks," she smiled, and drank it with little sips, watching him over the rim of her glass in a way that made him feel very uncomfortable.

"Er," he coughed. "Would you like to borrow another book?"

"No, thanks," she said.

"Oh. Er, well, then why did you come?"

"I just wanted to see you," she said with a beaming smile. "Do you mind?"

"N-no," he stammered.

"How do I look today?" she asked.

"V-very nice." This was ridiculous.

"Do you really think so?" she said happily, smoothing down her hair. "It was pretty hard going. I hadn't combed my hair for seventy-five years!" Her expression changed as she plucked at her cape. "I hate this old thing," she grumbled. "Do you realize, I never minded before what I looked like. But now I think you'd like me better in pretty clothes, wouldn't you?"

"I don't know," said Tony. "You couldn't fly without your cape."

"It's so unfair," she sighed. "Normal girls can wear what they like, it's only vampire girls who have to dress in crummy old things like this!" She bit her lip, and seemed to be thinking. "Can I ask you something?" she said finally.

"Of course," said Tony.

"What do you think of vampires?"

Tony wasn't prepared for this. "Oh, er, they're great!" he answered.

"And . . . vampire girls?"

"Vampire girls?" he hedged. "I only know one."

"Well, what do you think of me?" she asked.

"You're okay," he muttered, and felt himself blush.

Her face fell. "Only okay?" she said. "I think you're much, much better than okay." She stopped suddenly, and looked as if she were going to cry.

What was he going to do? The whole conversation had gotten out of hand, thought Tony, who wanted desperately to change the subject.

"Where is Rudolph?" he asked suddenly.

"All you ever think about is Rudolph," she said, sighing.

"That's not true," said Tony. "But he is going to pick up the cape tonight."

"Was going to," she said with a sniff.

"He isn't coming?"

"No. He can't. He's sick."

"Sick?" Tony sounded worried. "It wasn't . . . the night watchman?" he asked, a catch in his voice.

"No," she said. "Blood poisoning."

"Blood poisoning?" echoed Tony. That sounded like a very serious disease. "Where is he?"

"In his coffin with a temperature," she replied.

Tony did not know what to say. Poor Rudolph was lying alone in his coffin with no one to take care of him. When *he* was sick, his parents sent for the doctor and brought him soup and medicine to make him feel better.

"Could we go and see him?" he asked.

"See him?" giggled Anna. "And what if my parents saw *you*? Or my grandparents? Or my aunt?"

"Yes . . . er, well maybe we'd better not," agreed Tony, whose hair began to stand on end at the mere mention of the other vampires. "Is he *really* sick?"

"Are you worried he might die?" asked Anna. Tony nodded. "Well, forget it! He's dead already, remember."

Tony hadn't thought of that, but he didn't think that it made much difference. "Even so, he must be feeling rotten," he said. "We should take care of him."

"What does 'take care of' mean?" Anna asked. She had never heard that expression before.

" 'Taking care of' someone means you go and see someone and play games with them and read them a story and make them laugh." At least, that was what happened whenever he was sick. Tony wasn't sure what you did with vampires.

"No one takes care of us," said Anna. "My family are either all asleep in their coffins or out and . . . well, you know all about that." She sighed. "Anyway, nobody has any time for us. Nobody has ever read me a story or played a game with me."

Poor Anna, thought Tony. It must be really tough being a vampire kid. He always thought his parents paid little enough attention to him, but he had a fantastic time compared to a vampire.

"We could look after Rudolph, as long as your family weren't there," he suggested.

"Supposing one of them comes home early?" asked Anna.

Tony waved his hand nonchalantly. "That's not very likely," he said. "Anyway, I've already been to the vault once."

"What!" exclaimed Anna. "You've already been there?"

"Yeah, with Rudolph," said Tony.

"And no one found out?"

"No. Aunt Dorothy almost did, but I got into Rudolph's coffin just in time."

Anna breathed a sigh of relief. "Aunt Dorothy's the worst," she said. "She once tried to bite me, even though I'm a vampire too!"

"Ugh!" Tony could not stop himself. He felt his throat gingerly as he remembered Aunt Dorothy's booming voice echoing around the vault.

"But she's almost always out the longest," said Anna soothingly. "She's the greediest, you see. So—when are we going?"

Tony seemed to have lost his earlier enthusiasm. "Do you really think we should?"

"Yeah. Come on! You said yourself that we should be taking care of Rudolph."

"Okay. If you're sure."

"Come on," she urged. "You've got the other cape." She jumped up and down on the windowsill with impatience. "Rudolph will be surprised," she said, and laughed.

"I just hope he's all right," said Tony, joining her on the sill with the cape. And away they flew.

12 / Vampire Stories

"Do you know what story I like best out of your book?" asked Anna as they flew side by side through the night. "It's the one about the snow vampire."

"Which one's that?" asked Tony, who had not read all the stories.

"You know," said Anna, and with a dreamy look in her eyes, she began to tell it. "It all happens in the mountains in an old house miles from anywhere. After sunset each evening the curtains of every window that looks westward have to be kept drawn, and anyone who opens them better watch out!"

"Why?" asked Tony.

"Wait and see," said Anna, and her voice dropped to a whisper. "One day, when there are guests staying at the house, a snowstorm starts. One woman goes to the window and draws back the curtain. Outside she sees a white figure passing slowly in front of the house."

"The vampire," breathed Tony.

Anna nodded. "But the guests don't believe it's a vampire. They think it's someone who got lost in the blizzard. So one of them, a man, goes to the door to let him in. But no one is there. He steps outside to look around, and . . ."

"What happens?" asked Tony.

"The next morning they find the man. He's leaning up against a tree, dead, and around him are little spaces as if the wind had swept the snow aside."

"But really it was the snow vampire," said Tony.

"Exactly!"

"I like the one about the moth the best," said Tony. "It starts one stormy black night. There's this man, all by himself. Suddenly someone knocks at his door. He opens it, and standing there is a beautiful young woman. Her hair is jet black, and she has pointed ears and very red lips. Her voice is strange, deep and throaty." Anna giggled. "He invites her in, thinking she must be drenched to the bone. . . ."

"And of course she isn't!" interrupted Anna.

"No. She's completely dry. Anyway, the man has a dog. . . ."

"Ooh!" shuddered Anna.

"And when the dog sees the woman, it begins to howl and howl, so the man has to put it outside."

"And then?" asked Anna.

"The man comes back, and the woman asks him the way to the town. He says he'll show her the way, but when he gets his flashlight . . ."

"She's disappeared!" said Anna triumphantly.

Tony began to warm to his story. "The man tells a friend about his nocturnal visitor, and the friend warns him she's a vampire. But the man doesn't believe him. Instead, he asks him to look after his dog for a few days, because it won't come into the house."

"That was lucky," breathed Anna. "Vampires hate dogs."

"That evening the woman comes for the second time. She goes over to the man and puts her ice-cold hands around his neck. A strange heaviness comes over him, and suddenly he remembers the Bible he is holding in his lap."

"No!" exclaimed Anna. "No! Stop it!" Her eyes were wide open, and she stared at Tony in horror. "You don't mean that the man . . ."

"Beats the vampire?" finished Tony. "Yes. He drives a wooden something through her heart. Should I tell you what it was?" Tony was so deep in his story that he failed to notice the effect it was having on Anna.

"No," she whimpered. "No."

"A matchstick!" declared Tony. "She changed into a moth, and so a matchstick was all he needed for a wooden stake!" For the first time since he had begun his story, Tony turned and looked at Anna. She was deathly pale.

"Y-you meany," she cried, the tears running down her face. "You told me the whole thing just to upset me!"

"No, no, really," Tony tried to reassure her. "I never thought the matchstick part would frighten you."

She shook her head wordlessly and began to fly faster, so that Tony had difficulty keeping up. "Wait! I didn't mean it, really. I'm sorry."

But she only flew faster still, and soon disappeared from sight.

Now what was he going to do? Should he go on alone? Maybe she'd be waiting for him, and he did not like to think what a frightened vampire might do. Why didn't he just fly home? But that wouldn't be fair to Rudolph, who was sick in his coffin with blood poisoning. As these thoughts went through Tony's mind, he suddenly saw a small shadow coming toward him. At first he was frightened, but he recognized Anna.

"I've been thinking," she said. "I'm not mad at you anymore. Are we friends?"

"Of course," said Tony, relieved.

"Good!" She laughed, and took his hand. "Let's go then. We're almost there."

13 / First Aid

The wall of the cemetery was already in sight. The sky was clear, the moon shone brightly, and as a result the cemetery looked much less spooky and mysterious to Tony than it had the Sunday before. Maybe it was just that this was his third visit, he thought, as he followed Anna over the wall and landed in the grass on the other side.

"The entrance is right over there," Anna whispered, "but we have to wait to make sure everything's quiet."

Tony nodded. "I know," he said. "The night watchman."

"Ssh," she hissed.

Tony looked around at the tilted gravestones, almost overgrown by the long grass, the rusty old crosses sticking up out of the undergrowth, and the shadowy mass of the oak tree, under which lay the entrance to the vault.

Anna was straining her ears to catch the slightest sound. After a while she stood up. "Okay," she said. "We can go."

"Why don't you, er, go first?" suggested Tony, who suddenly felt nauseated.

Anna looked surprised. "Why? I promise there won't be anyone else in the vault besides Rudolph."

"But you could just make sure," insisted Tony. What if Aunt Dorothy had had another fainting fit? Or if one of the others had stayed behind to take care of Rudolph? Tony shuddered at the thought of coming face to face with Thelma the Thirsty.

"Oh, all right," said Anna. "I'll take a look. But you have to keep hidden." She vanished down into the hole, and Tony crept deeper into the shadows.

At that very moment he heard soft footsteps. They sounded far away, but in the stillness that enveloped the graveyard, there could be no doubt of their reality. An icy shudder ran through him. It couldn't be Robert, could it? But he would never have been able to follow them from the ground. No, there was only one explanation: the night watchman!

By now Tony could make out the figure of a man. He was fairly small, and he was moving swiftly but carefully, his head turning from this side to that. As he came nearer Tony could make out a gray, wrinkled

face with a pointed nose and bright restless little eyes,
all of which made him look a lot like a rat. Then
Tony's gaze was riveted to something else: out of the
pocket of his overalls poked an enormous hammer
and some sharp wooden stakes!

Tony hardly breathed. The deep shadow of the
oak tree hid him perfectly, so he felt he was fairly safe,
but Anna . . . at any moment she would pop her head
up to call him, and the night watchman was only a
few feet away! He had already turned those piercing
eyes on to the darkness under the oak tree.

Tony saw the stone at the entrance to the vault

begin to move, and suddenly he had an idea. He picked up a largish stone from the ground, and lobbed it as far as he could away from the oak tree. The stone landed heavily a ways away, and like a hound on the scent, the night watchman hurried off in the direction of the noise, baying: "Now I've got you!" Tony watched him start poking around in the bushes, brandishing the hammer and one of the wooden stakes. Tony raced over to Anna and slid down into the vault, pulling the stone over the entrance after him.

"Phew!" he gulped, leaning against the cool stone wall. "That was close!"

"What was?" asked Anna.

"The night watchman," said Tony, still out of breath. "He nearly caught you moving the stone."

"The night watchman?" gasped Anna. "Did you see him?"

"Yeah—but he didn't see me."

"Where is he now?"

Tony grinned. "Looking for a stone!"

"What?"

"I threw a stone to distract him, and now he's on a wild goose chase," explained Tony.

Anna breathed a sigh of relief. "Don't you think he looks like a rat?"

"Mmm," agreed Tony. "Hideous."

"I agree," said Anna, giggling. "We vampires look

really sweet in comparison. Do you know what his name is? Mr. McShrew."

"No!" Tony laughed.

"It is." Anna grinned delightedly and hopped from one foot to the other chanting: "Silly Mr. McShrew. You don't know where us vampires are, do you?"

A rasping cough from the vault interrupted them.

"Rudolph!" cried Tony. "How is he?"

"Him?" scoffed Anna. "He's all right. He's already walking around. But now Gruesome Gregory's got it."

"Gruesome Gregory?" Who was Gruesome Gregory? Of course, their older brother.

"Does he know that I'm . . . ?"

"Of course," said Anna, nodding. "But don't worry. We vampire kids stick together."

"He . . . er . . . won't do anything to me?"

"No!" said Anna, smiling. "At least not with us around."

They went down the steps. One candle was burning, and by its light they could see Rudolph sitting in his coffin reading, while in the coffin next to him a bigger, stronger vampire was tossing and turning. Rudolph looked up from his book and laid a finger across his lips. "He's asleep," he whispered, and motioned to them to come and sit on the edge of his coffin.

"What's wrong with him?" asked Tony.

"Flu," replied Rudolph, "and I'm not surprised, him out in the damp air every night."

Tony looked furtively at the slumbering form. A certain similarity with Rudolph was unmistakable, but Gruesome Gregory's face was paler and the hollows of his eyes even more pronounced. "He looks sick," said Tony.

"Mmm." Rudolph nodded. "Drained of blood, poor thing."

A deep growl came from Gregory, making Tony shrink back in fright. He hoped Anna had been right about how harmless her older brother was.

"I wanted to come and see you, Rudolph," he explained, "but since you're better . . ."

"You're not going already?" cried Anna.

"I-I ought to get back home," said Tony. "I forgot my key." He had to get out before Gregory woke up.

But already it was too late. Gruesome Gregory opened his eyes. He sat up, grumbling, and stared at Tony. "Who is this?" he asked in a menacing voice.

"Oh, Greg," crooned Anna. "This is Tony. Don't you remember, we told you about him."

"Oh, yes," said Gregory, sounding disappointed. "Tony. I'm hungry."

"You can go out again tomorrow," soothed Anna.

Gregory yawned. His mouth opened so wide that Tony could see the rows of gleaming pointed teeth; his eyeteeth were over an inch long! Tony shivered.

He wished he could get out of the vault, but of course the worst thing he could do would be to show he was frightened—that would make him easy prey.

Gregory was smiling now. "Don't come too close to me," he said. "You might catch something you don't want!"

"Er, yes," said Tony, who had no intention of getting any closer to Gregory. "Maybe it would be better if I went home."

"Why?" snickered Gregory. "Don't you like it here?"

"Y-yes," Tony protested, stuttering. "Of course I do. It's just that I don't want to get the flu."

"Let's play Parcheesi!" proposed Gregory, and he pulled a long box out of his coffin.

"Yeah, let's!" agreed Anna excitedly. "Come on, Rudolph, help me set up the board."

They brought a little coffin over from the wall and turned it over so that it made a perfect table between Gregory's coffin and the one next door. Gregory set out the board and they all gathered around, Tony still hesitating.

"I'll be blue," said Gregory.

"I call red!" said Anna.

"What color do you want?" Rudolph asked Tony.

"Oh, er, yellow," said Tony.

"Who's going to start?" asked Anna.

"Tony," said Gregory. "Guests are always allowed

to start." He pushed the dice over to Tony, who shook them and threw. It was a three.

"Bad luck," said Gregory with a gloating grin.

Now it was Rudolph's turn, which gave Tony a chance to really look at the board. It looked like a normal one, except that the starting points looked like coffins.

"How did you get the game?" he whispered to Anna.

"Uncle Theo found it for us," she replied.

"Found it?" asked Tony in disbelief. How could anyone just "find" a game?

"Well," she said, giggling, "maybe it would be better to call it 'booty.' "

Gregory had just taken his turn and had thrown a four. "Unfair!" he grumbled, and flung the dice away angrily. Rudolph ran after them and brought them back to the table. Now it was Anna's turn. She threw carefully, and they landed just at the edge of the board: double sixes!

"Doesn't count!" shouted Gregory. "The dice aren't flat."

"Are too!" stormed Anna. "They're flat on the board." Before she could pick up the dice to throw again, Gregory brought his fist crashing down on the coffin, so that the dice flew up in the air. Anna turned red with fury. "You can't *ever* lose, can you?" she fumed.

Gregory looked offended, but he didn't say anything. He lay back in his coffin with dignity, and shut his eyes. Rudolph shrugged his shoulders and began to look for the scattered pieces of the game, which he carefully put back in the box. Meanwhile, a contented snoring rose from the coffin.

"Is he asleep?" asked Tony.

Anna shook her head. "He's only pretending. But you better not disturb him."

"He's got a terrible temper," whispered Tony.

"Ssh," said Anna. "Don't get him worked up again. It's just a sign of puberty."

"Of what?" asked Tony.

"Growing up," explained Anna.

"Oh, I see." Tony thought of Gregory's grating voice, which seemed to change pitch constantly. "His voice is cracking?"

"Exactly," said Anna, "and that's why he's so moody. But the worst thing is that he'll never grow out of it. He died in puberty, and that's where he'll stay."

At that moment the stone at the entrance of the vault began to move. Gregory went on pretending to be asleep, but Rudolph was rooted to the spot, his eyes fixed in horror on the entrance. Anna pulled Tony to one side and whispered, "Hide, quick!"

"Where?" gasped Tony.

"In one of the coffins!"

"I'll go in Rudolph's," stammered Tony. At least he knew that one, and had managed to survive the revolting smell once already. He dreaded to think what horrors the other coffins might hold in store.

Anna helped him climb in, and then shut the lid. It was not a moment too soon: already there was the sound of hurrying feet coming down the steps, and a voice that Tony recognized only too well called: "Drat and botheration! This could only happen to me."

"What happened, Aunt Dorothy?"

"My false teeth!" she complained. "I must have left them behind in my coffin."

Tony heard her clattering across the vault.

"There they are," she said in relief. "Imagine if I'd lost them for good!" Apparently she had put them in place by now, for these last words sounded much more distinct.

"Well, I'll be on my way again," she declared. Then she stopped. "Rudolph, why aren't you in your coffin?"

"I'm feeling much better, Aunt," explained Rudolph.

"Nonsense! I'm sure you're not," insisted Aunt Dorothy. "What would your mother say? Get back into your coffin immediately!"

Tony's heart almost stopped beating.

Footsteps came nearer, the lid opened, and a figure climbed into the coffin. "You see?" hissed Rudolph.

"Plenty of room for two!" Out loud he called: "Good night, everyone!" and closed the lid. They heard Aunt Dorothy clatter back up the steps, and a minute later Anna announced that the coast was clear.

However, all that came from the coffin was a low moan. Anna opened the lid anxiously and saw Rudolph leaning over Tony, whose eyes were tightly closed. She called out, shocked. "Rudolph! You wouldn't hurt Tony!" Her cry woke Tony, who gave a yelp when he saw the vampire.

Slowly Rudolph lifted his head. "Have you all gone crazy?" he said calmly. "I was only giving Tony artificial respiration."

"Artificial respiration?" echoed Tony suspiciously, carefully feeling his neck; but there was not the slightest trace of a bite, and no blood either.

"You fainted," explained Rudolph, "and I thought I could—"

"Oh, you and your first-aid course!" scoffed Anna.

"I'm going," said Tony limply. His legs felt like rubber. He sat up slowly and climbed out of the coffin.

"Poor Tony," Anna said. "I'll take you home."

"Thanks," mumbled Tony.

Together they climbed the steps. They had nearly reached the top when Rudolph popped up next to them. He looked apologetic. "I'm sorry, Tony," he said shamefacedly. "I-I only wanted to help you. You don't really believe I'd . . ."

"No, of course not," said Tony, holding out his hand. "Forget it."

"Good," said Rudolph. "I thought you might have had enough of us."

"Come on, Tony!" called Anna. "We can go now."

"Okay, then," said Tony, turning in the narrow passage. "See you on Saturday." He never heard Rudolph's reply, because Anna had taken his hand and pulled him up into the fresh air.

14 / Anna's Idea

The clean night air restored Tony once more to his senses. He breathed in great gulps of it and stretched his stiff limbs. Anna watched him, smiling.

"Was it that bad?" she asked.

"In the coffin, you mean? No." At least it was over now, and he was safely out of the clutches of Gregory and Aunt Dorothy. "It was just a little narrow," he explained. "And—stuffy."

"Stuffy?" Anna giggled. "Well, what do you expect? We can't air them out, exactly. And as for these old capes..."

She stopped, looking worriedly around her as if something had just occurred to her. "We better get going," she whispered. "Who knows if old McShrew is lurking around the place."

"Have you seen him?"

"No. But we better not take any chances." She took off into the air, Tony following unsteadily.

"There was something I wanted to ask you," she said. "Are there any love stories about vampires?"

"Love stories?" Tony thought for a moment. "I can't think of any."

They flew along together without speaking. After a while Anna said dreamily, "I read one once that had a happy ending."

"Oh?" said Tony. "What happened?"

"Well, the boy ended up as a vampire too, and they both lived happily ever after."

"Yuk!" said Tony. "I don't call that a happy ending!"

"Don't you?" Anna looked at him with wide eyes. "Not even if it was with me?"

Tony was aware he would have to be careful. This was dangerous ground again. "Well, I can't ever become a vampire."

"Why not?" asked Anna. "If I . . ." She paused, realizing that maybe it wasn't exactly the right moment to initiate Tony into the finer points of how to become a vampire.

"Er, you see, as soon as I get my teeth I'll be able to—"

"I do *not* want to become a vampire!" interrupted Tony.

"You don't?" Anna could not believe it.

"No!" he said emphatically, annoyed that she thought he would. "And what's more, I don't have any intention of becoming one!"

He flew on ahead without looking back. It was not until he heard a sob from behind that he turned around.

"Y-you don't l-like me," she sniffed. "Y-you've got another g-girl friend."

"I do not," insisted Tony. "I promise."

"Really?"

"Really."

She sighed with relief and wiped her eyes with the back of her hand. "It doesn't matter if you're not a vampire," she said, "as long as we're friends." She began to smile again.

"We're almost there," said Tony, even though in fact there was another quarter of a mile to go. Why did Anna always have to start these embarrassing conversations? "I think I can see the lights," he continued, beginning to fly more quickly. He would not normally be in such a hurry to get home, but with Anna on his heels, it was a different story. He couldn't bear to think of what other questions she might dream up to ask him.

In the living room, his parents had turned on the television. Tony only hoped they hadn't noticed his absence, so he could simply creep into his own room.

"The window's shut!" hissed Anna, who could see much better than Tony in the dark.

"Oh, no!" Tony was upset. It was true. As they came nearer he could see that the windows were definitely locked from the inside. Not even the little one at the top was open.

"Now I'll have to ring the bell," he said worriedly, "and they'll find out everything."

"Say you went for a walk," suggested Anna.

"I'll tell them the truth," said Tony. "They'll never believe it anyway."

Anna went with him to the front door. Tony took off the cape and gave it to her. Suddenly she looked sad.

" 'Bye, Tony," she said softly, and without a backward glance she vanished into the night.

15 / Some Awkward Questions

As Tony went up in the elevator he tried to imagine what his parents would say. Would they be worried? Or furious? Or what? When he stepped out and saw that the door of the apartment was shut, he knew he was in for it. Normally when he rang the buzzer downstairs, there was someone standing at the open doorway to welcome him.

He pushed the door bell and waited. He heard his mother's footsteps approaching, and the door opened.

"Do you know how late it is?" was her greeting.

"Nine o'clock?" Tony hazarded hopefully.

"It's a quarter to ten!" his mother shouted. "We've been waiting for you since eight o'clock. You've got some explaining to do, young man!" She marched him back to the living room, where his father was sitting on the sofa. When Tony came in, he stood up and turned off the television. Things were really looking bad.

"Where have you been?" asked his father.

"Me? Oh, just out for a walk." Tony tried to sound innocent.

"I see. For a walk. At nine thirty at night, my ten-year-old son gets it into his head to go for a walk." He paused, then added sarcastically, "And may one inquire where His Lordship walked to?"

"Er, oh, here and there."

"An illuminating piece of information." The corners of his father's mouth had begun to twitch, which meant that he was getting very, very angry, and trying to hide it.

"There's such a funny smell," said his mother suddenly. "Is it you, Tony?" Tony felt himself being scrutinized from head to toe, and involuntarily he too glanced down, hoping that there was no telltale sign of where he'd been, like earth from the cemetery on his shoes. Luckily there wasn't.

"Have you been burning something?" asked his mother.

"No," said Tony. Here it comes, he thought to himself.

"Maybe somebody else made a fire, and you were 'just looking'?"

"No."

"Have you been smoking?"

"No."

"Why do you smell of smoke then?"

"Got me. Maybe it was Anna."

"Anna?" His parents' ears pricked up. "Who is Anna?"

"A girl friend."

"A *what*?"

"She's Rudolph's sister."

"*Whose* sister?" shouted his father. "Did you say Rudolph's?"

"Yes," said Tony, who could not understand why his father was so upset.

"Are you sure you're telling the truth?" asked his father.

"Yes," protested Tony.

"Okay. We'll find out."

"Are you going to call up?" asked Tony's mother. Dad nodded, and opened the telephone book. "Ah, here we are. Appleby, Henry."

"Who is Henry Appleby?" asked Tony warily. His father threw him a look.

"Well, well. Imagine you not knowing who Appleby is," he said, dialing the number. Someone at the other end of the phone must have answered almost immediately, because he continued in quite a different voice: "Mr. Appleby? It's Noodleman here. I'm sorry to disturb you; there's just a little matter I'd like to clear up. My son here claims that your daughter

Anna . . . What? You haven't . . . ?" He paused. "I see. Thank you very much. Good night."

He put down the receiver and turned to Tony. "Did you know that your friend Rudolph doesn't have a sister? He's only got a brother, and his name is Leo."

"Leo?" asked Tony.

"And as for so-called Rudolph—he's not called Rudolph at all, or even Rudolph Robert, but just plain, simple Robert."

"Robert?" Tony was confused. Then suddenly light dawned: they must be talking about the Robert he had managed to smuggle over in Rudolph's place. A terrible thought occurred to him: after all, Robert's nickname was Blabbermouth. Maybe he had called Tony's parents and blown it all? He could hardly believe that Robert would be such a traitor.

"Well?" asked his father. "What have you got to say?"

"I've always called him Rudolph," said Tony.

"And his sister?"

"She's called Anna, like I said."

"Tony! Haven't I just told you Robert hasn't got a sister?"

"Rudolph has," said Tony stubbornly.

At this point his mother decided to try the rational approach. "Tony," she said, "you must see that it seems very strange to us. You say you have been out for a walk with a girl who simply doesn't exist. Can't you tell us the truth?"

"I don't know what to say anymore," said Tony, sighing.

"All right then," said his father, who was having to make a visible effort to control himself. "I recognized your so-called 'Rudolph.' He's the son of a colleague of mine at work, and he's called Robert Appleby, not Rudolph Sackville-Bagg."

"Why didn't you say so before?" asked Tony.

His father gasped for air. "Because I wanted to hear what you had to say about it."

At least Tony now knew what was going on.

"It seems that we still haven't met the real Rudolph," added Tony's mother slowly. "I believe there really is someone called Rudolph, with a sister called Anna. But why haven't you let us meet him?"

Tony had to smile. His mother's cool, thoughtful approach had brought her a lot closer to the truth than all his father's rantings and ravings.

"You see," he explained, "you kept bothering me to bring Rudolph home. But Rudolph didn't want to come, so I asked Robert instead. By the way," he added as an afterthought, "I really didn't know that Robert's last name was Appleby."

"Why didn't Rudolph want to come?" asked his mother.

"Because he always stays up so late, so he's sleepy,

and also he doesn't like cake. He's kind of weird."

His mother laughed. "That doesn't matter. I enjoy meeting weird people. And if he doesn't want to eat anything, he doesn't have to."

"He'd be embarrassed," said Tony. "And also, he stinks."

At this, even his father laughed. "You certainly know how to pick your friends!" he said.

"He doesn't really know how to behave," continued Tony.

"That doesn't matter either," said his mother. "What really counts in a person is their heart, and I'm sure your Rudolph has a good heart, Tony."

Tony blanched. "A good heart? What do you mean?" he said. Had Mom guessed what Rudolph was like?

But her face was all smiles. "I mean, he's someone you can depend on," she explained. "Someone who won't leave you when the going gets tough."

"Oh, um, yes." Tony was very relieved.

"If you like him," continued his mother, "I think we would like him too."

"Do you think so?" Tony sounded doubtful. "So, do you like vampires?"

"You're not starting that vampire business again, are you?" his father said, and laughed.

His mother looked angry. "I don't think it's very funny," she said.

Dad laughed even more loudly. "So when do we get to meet this famous vampire of yours?" he asked.

"Um, I'll have to ask him," said Tony. "Next week, maybe?" He suddenly felt exhausted, and was dying to be able to creep into bed.

"You better keep your window shut," called his mother as he reached the door. "There have been the most horrible bats flying around in the last few weeks. Not that they'd come inside or anything, but—"

"Okay, okay," said Tony, turning around quickly so his parents wouldn't see his smile. "Good night."

16 / A New Member of the Family

In the middle of the night Tony woke up. He rubbed his eyes and blinked. Where on earth was he? A moment before he had been sitting at a long table with all the vampires, and Sabina the Sinister had been making a speech. . . . But now he seemed to be in his own bed.

He could hear the ticking of his alarm clock near his pillow, and the outline of his desk and lamp showed up clearly against the pale patch of light that marked the window. Tony breathed a sigh of relief. For a second he had really believed he was in the graveyard at an important vampire ceremony.

He tried to remember. Yes, that was it: A new vampire was being welcomed into the family. The vault had been decorated for the occasion: black candles were burning in tall silver candlesticks, and the coffins had been pushed together to form a table, which had been covered with a black cloth. At the head sat Sabina the Sinister, with the other vampires lined up along the sides according to rank: on her right sat Frederick the Frightful, Thelma the Thirsty, Aunt Dorothy, and Uncle Theodore; on her left, William the Wild, Gruesome Gregory, Rudolph, and Anna the Toothless. And next to Anna was—Tony himself! Only then did he realize what was happening.

Sabina the Sinister had already gotten to her feet, and after clearing her throat a couple of times and baring her terrible teeth, she began: "My dear kinsmen, it gives me great pleasure to introduce to you a new member of the family." She paused dramatically, raised her hand, and pointed at Tony. All nine pairs of eyes swiveled to rest upon him. And what terrible, hungry eyes they were.

"All our thanks go to Anna, who has won Tony for us," continued Sabina, and all the vampires thumped on the coffins with their fists to show their appreciation. "And now it is our duty and pleasure to make Tony into a real vampire." At this the vampires leaped to their feet. As if given a signal, they began to roll their eyes and gnash their teeth with the most terrifying clacking. Slowly, very slowly, they came closer to Tony. Sabina the Sinister reached him first, and stretched out her long fingers with their talonlike nails to fasten on his neck—but before she could touch him . . . Tony woke up.

He sat up in bed and looked at the alarm clock. Three o'clock. He lay back down again with a sigh and closed his eyes. He just hoped he wouldn't have another dream like that one.

17 / Nosy Parents

"You haven't been very wide awake today, have you?" commented Tony's father the following evening. They were sitting on the couch waiting for the beginning of a wildlife documentary on television.

Tony yawned. "I think I'll go to bed," he said.

"Your 'walk' yesterday must have tired you out," teased his father.

"Actually, it was my math homework," corrected Tony. Whoever said school days were the happiest days of your life?

"Could you do it all?" asked his mother.

"Of course," replied Tony.

Just then the telephone rang. Tony's father picked up the receiver. "Noodleman here," he said in his special telephone voice. Then a puzzled look came over his face. "Who did you want to speak to? Are you

sure you've got the right number? Hold on a minute."
He covered the receiver with his hand. "It's some
crazy girl," he whispered. "I can hardly understand
what she's saying. She hisses. Is it some kid from
school?"

"Can't be," said Tony's mother, quickly taking the
receiver from him. "It's Mrs. Noodleman. Who's
speaking please? Who? You want to talk to Tony?"
Her forehead wrinkled in disbelief. "It's for you," she
whispered.

"Who is it?" asked Tony's father.

Mom shrugged her shoulders. "I have no idea. She
spoke as if she had her hand over her mouth."

By this time Tony had the receiver in his hand.
"Hello?" he said. A soft giggle came from the other
end. "Who is it?" he asked.

"Anna!" came the answer, soft and squeaky but
quite clear.

Tony turned pale. "Y-you?" he stammered. This
was just great! To make matters worse, he had a
parent on either side of him, listening to every word.

"Who is it?" demanded his father.

"Anna." It was an unwilling reply.

"What does she want?" hissed his mother.

"I don't know," said Tony through clenched teeth.
"I haven't had a chance to find out."

"Are you still mad at me?" Anna was asking.
"About yesterday? Because I know I . . ."

"No, no, of course not," Tony reassured her.

"I've got a surprise for you," she said.

"A surprise?" Out of the corner of his eye he saw his parents exchange a meaningful look. "What sort of surprise?" he asked.

"A story," she said. "A real vampire love story." At these last words, she was so overcome with giggles that Tony could hardly hear her. "Can I come around and read it to you this evening?"

"Um, no, not this evening. Tomorrow maybe."

"Okay. Tomorrow. What time?"

Tony glanced at his parents and thought for a minute. "My grandmother has nine clocks," he said, and was pleased to see the look of complete bewilderment that passed between them. Serve them right for eavesdropping!

Luckily Anna had understood. "At nine o'clock. Okay."

"What's Rudolph doing?"

"He's already gone," explained Anna. "He was starving."

"Oh, I see." As always when the vampires' eating habits were mentioned, Tony felt sick. "Well, say hi to him for me," he said. Why did his parents have to stand so close to him? Why couldn't they go into the kitchen for a while?

" 'Bye," he said.

"See you tomorrow," said Anna, and hung up.

"What? Finished already?" said Dad in mock astonishment.

"Yes," growled Tony.

"What was that you said about Grandma having nine clocks?" asked his mother.

"Oh, just a joke."

"Why didn't you invite Anna over when Rudolph comes?" his father wanted to know.

"I didn't think of it."

"What about Rudolph?" asked his mother. "Have you decided when yet?"

"No. I haven't seen him."

"Doesn't he go to school?"

Tony had to laugh. "No," he said.

"Oh?" His mother was very surprised.

"He has a . . . tutor," said Tony. He had read somewhere that you could have a tutor instead of going to school.

"My goodness! Is he sick?" asked his mother.

"No, not exactly. But he sleeps too late to go to school."

His mother shook her head incredulously. "What some kids get away with!" she said.

"I agree," said Dad with a smile. "Amazing."

"I'm glad you think so," said Tony angrily, and went out, slamming the door behind him. First they eavesdrop, then they interrogate him, and now they laugh at him. No wonder he was mad!

18 / Rendezvous in Pajamas

The following evening Tony was ready for bed unusually early. He had already washed up and was in his pajamas by eight thirty.

"You're not going to bed already, are you?" His mother was shocked.

"I want to read," explained Tony.

"All right. But lights out at nine, remember?"

"Okay. Good night."

Once in his room Tony half-closed the curtains. He took down his new book, *Tales of the Otherworld*, from his shelf, climbed into bed, and began to read. The first story was perfect for his mood: it was about two boys who went to a lonely inn one night and . . .

Soft footsteps crossed the hall, and Tony jerked upright. Then he remembered it was only his mother coming to see if he was still reading, and he quickly hid the book under his pillow and pretended to be asleep. The door opened quietly and closed again almost immediately. The footsteps went back across the hall. That meant he could relax and forget about his parents, because they thought he was asleep. He settled himself comfortably again, turned the light back on, then pulled out his book and looked for the right page.

A sudden tapping on the window made him jump. Outside he could only see a faint shadow. He put down the book and went to the window. There on the sill sat Anna. Tony pushed the curtain to one side and opened the window.

"Hi, Tony," said Anna, slipping into the room as noiselessly as a cat.

"Hello," replied Tony, feeling himself blush. It was a good thing it was dark.

"Do I smell nice?" she asked happily, beaming at him.

"Oh, uh, yes," murmured Tony. What else could he say? She would not be happy if he said she smelled of a mixture of dead leaves, moth balls, and mildew.

"It's my special perfume," she explained. "It's called Fragrant Earth."

"I've never heard of that before," said Tony.

"That's not surprising," Anna said proudly. "My mother makes it herself. It's only for vampires." With these words she came up close to Tony and bared her neck. "Can you smell it? Isn't it devilishly delicious?"

"Mmm," said Tony evasively. He hadn't smelled anything so revolting in his life. "It's . . . er, very powerful."

"Isn't it?" she agreed. "We're only allowed to wear it on very special occasions."

"It reminds me of onions," went on Tony, whose eyes were beginning to water.

"Its main ingredient is onions," said Anna. "Then you mix in a bit of deadly nightshade, and some cow dung."

"Ugh!" Tony could not stop himself.

Anna looked hurt. "I thought you liked it," she said.

"Oh, yes, I do," said Tony quickly. "It's just kind of unusual."

"Should we turn on some music?" suggested Anna, changing the subject.

Tony looked nervously at the door. "Better not," he said. "Mom and Dad think I'm asleep."

"Oh." She sounded disappointed. Then she brightened. "Never mind. I brought you something to read. A real vampire love story." She reached under her cape and pulled out a bundle of yellowing pages, which she smoothed carefully. Tony noticed they were covered with round, childish handwriting.

"Did you write it?" he asked.

Anna looked embarrassed. "Yes," she admitted, and began to read: "Once upon a time there were a king and queen who wanted to have a child—but in vain. But one day the queen was swimming in a pool, and it so happened that a frog hopped out of the water onto the edge and said: 'Your wish will come true.' And sure enough, before a year had passed, the queen gave birth to a baby boy. The joyful parents decided to have a feast to celebrate. In addition to all their friends and relatives, they invited the fairies to bring their son luck. But there were thirteen fairies in the kingdom, and the queen only had twelve golden plates, so one fairy didn't get an invitation. The feast was the most magnificent anyone could remember, and at the end, each fairy gave the child a gift: one blessed him with health, one with intelligence, another with good looks, and so on, until eleven had given him their blessing. At that second the thirteenth fairy, the one who had not been invited, burst into the hall and cackled: 'This is my gift! When he is fifteen, your son will prick his finger on a spindle and fall down dead!' Luckily the twelfth fairy had not given her gift yet, and even though she could not take away the spell completely, she was able to lessen its effect. 'He will not die,' she said, 'but he will fall into a deep sleep which will last for a hundred years.'"

"Oh?" said Tony. "A hundred years?" The story was becoming familiar.

"The king decided to protect his son from this fate, and so he gave the order that every spindle in the kingdom should be burned. It so happened that, on the prince's fifteenth birthday, the king and queen were away from the palace. The boy decided to explore, and finally found himself at the foot of an old turret. He climbed the narrow staircase and reached a tiny door at the top. In the lock was a rusty key, and as he turned it, the door sprang open and there, in a little room, sat an old woman spinning flax. 'What is that, bobbing up and down?' asked the prince. He took the spindle to see for himself, and at once the magic spell was fulfilled: he pricked his finger and fell on the nearby bed in a deep sleep. At that moment everyone else in the palace was overtaken by the same sleep. The king and queen had just gotten home, and they fell asleep. The entire court fell asleep. Even the horses in the stable, the dogs in the yard, the pigeons on the rooftop, and the flies on the walls, everything slept.

"A hedge of thorns grew up around the castle, growing higher every year so that soon nothing could be seen of the palace behind it. Tales of the handsome young prince were spread abroad in the land, and from time to time, princesses came to try to break through the hedge. They were never successful, however, for the thorn branches were twisted together like linked hands, where the princesses got stuck and died a terrible death. At last, after many years, a certain princess happened to come to that part of the country. An old man told her the story of the castle behind the wall of thorns, and the princess declared: 'I'm not afraid! I shall try to reach this handsome prince.' What the old man did not know was that this particular princess was in fact a vampire. She turned herself into a bat and flew over the hedge. Once in the courtyard of the castle, she saw the dogs and horses lying fast asleep, and venturing farther inside, she found the entire court sleeping too. Finally she came to the tower with the little room where the king's son lay. He was so handsome that she could not take her eyes off him, and she bent down and gave him a vampire kiss. He stirred and opened his eyes and looked at her happily. It did not take long before he was a vampire too, and the pair of them lived happily ever after."

"I know that story," said Tony. "It's the same as 'Sleeping Beauty.'"

"My version's better, though," said Anna.

"You forgot the court," said Tony, "and the king and queen. Did they turn into vampires also?"

"I haven't decided yet," said Anna. "I wanted to ask you about it. You don't think that would make it too grisly?"

"Why should it?" asked Tony. "After all, no one believes in vampire tales these days. . . ."

"What?" said Anna furiously. "No one believes in vampires? What about you? Don't you believe in us?"

"Oh, yes, I do, of course," Tony reassured her. "But everyone else . . ."

"Everyone else? I thought everyone was frightened of us."

"Sorry." Tony shook his head. "Last week, for instance, we had to write a composition. The title was 'A Terrifying Experience.' I went up to our teacher and asked her whether we were allowed to write about vampires, and she just laughed. 'Vampires?' she said, loud enough for the whole class to hear. 'Vampires belong to fairy tales, Tony. No, now you are in the fifth grade, and you should write about something that really happened.'"

"What an old crab!" snorted Anna. "What did you write about finally?"

"Something I saw on TV once."

"Did she notice?"

"No, she thought it was lively and realistic, and gave me ninety out of a hundred."

"Huh!" said Anna. "You'd have gotten a hundred for a vampire story. What about your parents? Don't they believe in us?"

Tony shook his head. "Not a bit. But they would like to meet you. You've been invited over."

"Really?" Anna's face lit up. "At last I'll be able to

meet your parents, Tony!" She clapped her hands and gave a little jump. "Are they as nice as you?"

"Um, I guess so." Tony was embarrassed.

"When can we come?"

"Next Wednesday?" suggested Tony. It was the first day that came into his head. "Do you think Rudolph will come too?"

"I'll ask him right away," she said, and jumped up onto the windowsill. " 'Bye then. See you on Wednesday."

"W-wait a minute," stuttered Tony. "Are you really going to come?"

"You bet!" she smiled, and vanished.

19 / Final Preparations

"Come on, Tony," said his mother the following Wednesday. "Help me whip this cream."

"It's much too early still," said Tony.

"Nonsense!" declared his mother. "It's almost four o'clock."

"That makes no difference. They always have an afternoon rest."

His mother gave him a searching look. "I'm sure even you don't really believe that."

"Yes, I promise it's true. It's good for their health." What a pain. He didn't think vampires ever got up before sunset, and that would mean they might not get there until eight o'clock. And Mom was already putting out the milk and cookies.

"Uh, Mom," began Tony. "I think I should explain, er, they might not come until eight o'clock."

"Come on now, Tony," said his mother. "It's almost your bedtime at eight."

"I know," replied Tony.

"Well, don't Rudolph and Anna have to go to bed also?"

"No," said Tony, trying not to laugh.

"What a way to bring up kids," grumbled his mother. "What's going to happen to all this food?" She waved a hand vaguely in the direction of the table. "Everything's all set up."

"I could have a snack now, and then have some apple juice later on after dinner," suggested Tony.

"What about getting up for school tomorrow morning?"

"Oh, come on, Mom, just this once," pleaded Tony.

"Well, all right," she agreed. "But I'm not at all pleased, and I'm only saying yes because I'm dying to meet these strange friends of yours."

Tony gave a quiet sigh of relief.

"What about all these cookies?" she went on.

"I'll eat them," offered Tony. His mother had bought his favorite kind again, and this time they were all for him! At least it would make up for the last time, when Robert had downed them all, and he had not had any.

"You may have one. You don't want to spoil your dinner," said his mother. "Then we'll have the rest later this evening."

"Great!" Tony could hardly believe his luck. Not only had his mother agreed to let him stay up late, but now he was getting an extra cookie.

"Here, you can have some milk too," said his mother, handing him a glass.

"Mmm, thanks." Tony took the milk and cookie and went off to his room. He had already finished his homework, so he could read in peace—and in just about four hours, the party would begin.

20 / A Lively Evening

Shortly after eight the front doorbell rang. Tony had been looking at the clock every few minutes for the past half hour, and now a shiver of expectancy ran through him. He hoped everything would be okay, and that Rudolph really had come also. What would his parents say? Tony was so excited that his legs almost wouldn't carry him out of his room.

His parents had already opened the door. "Good evening," he heard Rudolph say in his grating voice, followed almost immediately by Anna's piping: "Hello!"

"Welcome!" replied his mother, taking a couple of steps backward. "Come in."

"So here you are at last!" Dad was doing his best to sound nice, but it wasn't coming easily.

He had a good reason: Rudolph and Anna were a

sight to behold. They had put rouge on their cheeks and smeared red lipstick on their lips. Their faces, which were normally chalk white, were caked with brownish powder, but it had been put on in patches, so that there were still places where white gleamed through. The penetrating smell of Fragrant Earth hung pungently about the pair of them.

"This is for you," said Rudolph, holding out a bunch of greenery to Tony's mother.

"Thank you," she murmured, fingering the stems carefully. They had clearly been torn from a hedge somewhere.

"Aren't they pretty?" said Anna. "There are plenty like that growing at home."

"Ssh!" Rudolph hissed at her furiously. It was clear even to Tony that the sprigs were from the hedge that grew in the cemetery.

"I'll go and put them in water," said his mother, disappearing into the kitchen.

"Where is Tony, I wonder?" said Dad.

"Here," replied Tony, who had been watching their meeting from a distance.

"Tony!" said Anna, her face reddening. "How are you?"

"Oh, I'm fine," said Tony, and he blushed an equally deep crimson.

"Hello, Tony," said Rudolph, shaking him by the hand. Rudolph's hand felt cold and bony, like the hand of a skeleton. It was the first time that Tony had ever touched Rudolph's hand, and it made him shiver. Maybe it was because they both looked so strange and unfamiliar tonight. They must have come straight from the vault, in which case they could not have had anything to eat. In fact, Rudolph was looking pretty drained and weak.

"Uh, are you hungry?" Tony asked.

"Yes," said Rudolph. "Very."

"Come on in then," said Tony's father, trying to sound jovial. "Everything's ready. There are some cookies and fruit juice." He led the way into the living room.

"Is there milk, too?" whispered Anna. Tony nodded.

His parents had laid the table with the best china and decorated it with paper napkins and candles— everything looked beautiful, except the two visitors. The same thought must have occurred to Anna, who looked embarrassed and wandered uncertainly around the table.

"It looks so pretty!" she said. "We never have any-thing like this at home."

"Ssh!" said Rudolph, frowning.

"Why shouldn't I say that?" argued Anna. She turned to Tony's father and said, "It's true. We al-ways eat out."

"Do you?" said Tony's mother conversationally,

returning with the sprigs in a vase. "It must get very expensive to eat out all the time."

"Actually it's cheap." Rudolph could not help smiling, and for a moment his pointed teeth were revealed. He quickly covered his mouth with his hand.

"Those plants do smell strange," remarked Tony's father. "Should I open a window?"

"No, I wish you wouldn't," said Mom. "I'm sort of scared of those bats."

"Bats?" said Rudolph. "I love bats."

"Well, I don't," said Tony's mother firmly.

"They have the greatest faces."

"Ugh!" She shivered.

"Or vampires!" Anna could not resist the suggestion, and this time it was too much for Rudolph. He broke out laughing, but since his hand was still over his mouth, he ran out of air and began to choke.

"Are you all right?" asked Mom, but Rudolph could only cough.

"Wait a minute!" said Tony's mother, and ran to the kitchen, returning with a glass of water. "Drink this, you'll feel much better."

By this time Rudolph was coughing so badly that he didn't notice that Tony's mother was holding a glass to his lips. But he had barely tasted the first drop before he sprang up and ran into the hallway, sneezing and spluttering.

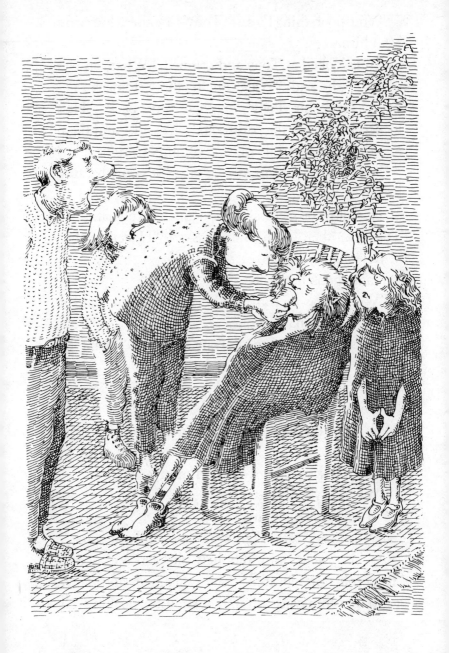

"You poor thing!" said Tony's mother, hurrying after him.

Anna looked at Tony and grinned. "What can you expect?" she said. "Water on an empty stomach . . ."

At this point Tony's mother came back. "He's locked himself in the bathroom," she said, "and there are the most terrible noises coming from inside."

To soothe her, Anna said calmly, "It's only because he's so hungry."

This did not seem a very adequate explanation to Tony's mother, but his father asked, "Haven't either of you had anything to eat?"

Anna shook her head.

"Well, come on, come on." He held out the plate of cookies and Anna took one.

"Go on, then," urged Tony's father. "Don't be shy."

"I, um, don't like cookies," she said.

"Oh. Well, never mind," said Tony's father.

"Would you like some apple juice?" asked Tony's mother.

"No, thank you. It gives me a tummyache."

"What do you like to drink then?"

"Milk, if you have any."

"Of course," said Tony's mother. "I'll get some."

As she went into the hall she let out a cry. "Rudolph's disappeared!" she exclaimed, and Tony heard her hurrying around anxiously, opening all the doors. "How could he have gotten out of the apartment?"

"Through the front door?" suggested Dad helpfully.

"No!" wailed Mom. "We would have noticed him."

"Maybe we just weren't looking at the right time?"

"Don't be ridiculous!" insisted Mom. "He would have had to have gone right past the living room door."

"Well, he must have flown then," said Dad angrily.

"Who knows?" said Mom. "Tony's bedroom window is open."

"What?" exclaimed Tony. *He* hadn't opened it. But of course he'd better not let the others know that. "Oh, yes, I left it open," he added.

"There you have it. A perfectly reasonable explanation," said his father.

If he only knew. Mom had almost hit the nail on the head, as usual.

"I suppose I just haven't looked in the right place," said Mom in a small voice, sitting down once more.

Dad turned to Anna. "Your brother can't fly, can he?" he asked.

"Of course not!" said Anna.

"I knew it. You see, Hilary? You and your crazy ideas."

Tony's mother looked at Anna warily. Tony

wondered if she was suspicious; his father would never notice a thing, but Mom was different. . . .

"May I have my milk?" asked Anna.

"Oh, of course. I forgot," said Tony's mother. "Tony, be a good boy and go get it." Grudgingly Tony got to his feet.

"Milk is very good for you," said Anna. "It makes you strong."

Tony returned with the milk and put the glass down in front of her. "Thank you." She smiled and emptied the glass in one gulp.

For a minute, nobody said anything. Then Dad remarked, "So you have a costume too?"

"Yes," nodded Anna, not at all surprised.

"Where do you have all these Halloween parties?"

"In private," said Anna. Tony looked at her admiringly. He would never have thought of such a good answer on the spur of the moment like that.

"I'd like to see what you look like without your costume on," said Tony's father.

Tony's heart nearly stopped beating, but Anna simply shrugged her shoulders casually and said, "Oh, not much different. Maybe a little prettier."

"Prettier?" Tony's father laughed hollowly. "At least you're not vain."

"No," agreed Anna.

"Or shy."

Anna looked at Tony. "Sometimes I am," she said.

"So you and your brother always go to these parties together?"

"Yes. We do almost everything together."

"Don't you ever fight?"

"Of course. He has a very old-fashioned outlook on certain things."

"Really? Such as?"

"Oh—anything to do with girls. He thinks boys are tougher than girls."

"Aren't they?" asked Dad.

"Don't tell me you agree with him?" said Anna, her face turning red.

"No, no," soothed Tony's father, "but you must admit most girls would rather wear pretty dresses than go climbing trees and getting themselves dirty."

"No, you've got it all wrong!" said Anna fiercely. "Why do girls wear pretty dresses? Only because their mothers like to dress them up. And then they don't climb trees because they're not supposed to get their clothes messed up."

"Exactly," agreed Tony's mother.

"But what about boys?" continued Tony's father. "Boys play with cars, and girls play with dolls."

Anna looked exasperated. "You just don't understand," she said.

"What do you think, Tony?" asked his father.

Tony hesitated. "I think girls are stupid," he said finally, "the ones who are always giggling and getting knocked over, even when they're just playing kick-ball!"

"Well, I think boys who say girls can't play kick-ball are dumb too!" declared Anna.

"Is your brother like that?" asked Tony's mother.

Anna nodded. "Even though the first of our line was a woman."

"What did you say? The first in your line? Are you just teasing us?" joked Dad.

Tony froze. Now Anna really had gone too far. But no, she was not so easily disturbed. "I meant our first ancestor," she explained. "She was called Cleo Hermione Victoria Charlotte Sabina Sackville-Bagg, the vampire."

"That's a very wonderful-sounding name," said Tony's father.

"It's too long," said Anna, "so it's been shortened."

"Your family sounds like an odd lot," said Tony's father, laughing.

"Do you think so?" Anna looked insulted. "Most people who have anything to do with us don't think we're the least bit odd."

"Really?" probed Dad. "What *do* they think of you?"

"I would prefer not to tell you," said Anna with dignity. "And now, I must be going." She stood up and smoothed her cape.

"You'll come over again soon, won't you?" asked

Dad. "Tony will be so sad if you don't," he added mischievously.

"Really?" asked Anna, looking tenderly at Tony. "Well, in that case . . ." She began to blush and ran out into the hall.

"Wait a minute!" called Dad. "You're going the wrong way. The front door's on the left!"

"Oh, of course." Anna sounded rather surprised. Out of habit, she had automatically turned in the direction of Tony's bedroom and the open window. Pulling herself together, she said good-bye, marched out of the front door, and went all the way down to the ground floor in the elevator.

Epilogue

"What a nice girl," said Tony's father when they were all around the table again. "Did you like her, Hilary?"

"I thought she was sort of strange."

"Strange? Why?"

"Her pale little face . . . the funny cape . . . her voice . . . I don't know."

"What about Rudolph?"

"He was even worse! Those bloodshot eyes and bony fingers."

"But they're only children." Dad laughed. "You sound as if you were frightened out of your wits, dear."

"What wits?" Tony laughed too.

His father looked at him sharply. "We don't want any of your cracks," he said sternly. "You were the one who brought up all this vampire nonsense."

"I did not!" answered Tony. "Vampires have been around since the Middle Ages."

"Oh yes? How do you know?"

"I read it in a book."

"In one of your horror stories, I suppose."

"No, actually, in a dictionary."

"Really?" asked Tony's mother, sounding genuinely interested. "I'd like to see that myself. Is it in ours?"

"No," answered Tony, "in the one at school."

"Well, it might be in ours too," said his mother hopefully, going over to the bookcase. She took out a book, leafed through it, and read: " 'Vampires: according to myth, these are bodies of the dead, who leave their coffins at night to suck the blood of humans.' "

"Yes, yes, we know all that," interrupted Tony's father. "There are other things according to myth, like..."

" ... witches, dwarfs, ghosts, and fairies," chanted Tony, who remembered only too well the first conversation he had had with his parents on the subject of vampires.

"So you see, there's nothing to worry about," reassured Dad, "unless you're going to believe in dwarfs and fairies, also."

"Of course I'm not," said Mom.

"And probably Rudolph and Anna will try to look

a little more normal when they come next time, won't they, Tony?"

"Mmm," said Tony doubtfully.

"Well, as far as I'm concerned, I'd be glad if it were a while before they came again," said Mom.

"I'm sure Tony won't agree," laughed Dad.

"I don't," said Tony. He had almost choked on his juice. "I guess now you're going to tell me never to play with Rudolph and Anna again?"

"No, no, we wouldn't go as far as that," said his mother, "but we *can* have our own opinion about your friends, can't we?"

"I guess so," Tony had to agree.

"I think they're creepy," said Mom, "and if there really were such things as vampires, I'm sure they would look just like your two friends!"

Dad laughed, as though Mom had cracked a good joke. "But there aren't such things as vampires," he said. "They're nothing more sinister than two normal kids who have dug a bit too deeply into their grandmother's closet." He took a cookie and munched on it, and for a while nobody said anything.

Then Tony grumbled. "Well, it was you who kept wanting to meet them, anyway. I warned you about them."

"Yes, I must admit, you did," said his mother, smiling. "Oh, well, I suppose I'll get used to them eventually."

"And you won't keep bringing up this vampire nonsense, will you, Tony?" said Dad.

Tony grinned. "Okay," he said. Poor old Dad still didn't have a clue, and Mom's suspicions would soon disappear. All had turned out just fine in the end.

"I'm going to bed," he said. "Good night."

"Good night, dear," replied his parents.

It was with a feeling of great contentment and satisfaction that Tony finally climbed into bed and pulled the covers up over his head.

About the Author

Angela Sommer-Bodenburg is the author of numerous short stories that have appeared in magazines and anthologies throughout the world, as well as several collections of poetry. Like the hero of *My Friend the Vampire*, Ms. Sommer-Bodenburg loves horror stories and has written a sequel, *The Vampire Moves In*, which will be published as an Archway Paperback.